Picture Me Yours

A BERKSHIRE ROMANCE

E.A. BRADY

SANDGATE EAST PUBLISHING

Dedication

For my family. Because everyone should have cheerleaders like these people!

I couldn't do any of this without their support and encouragement.

Sage

Sage had talked about everything else she could think of to avoid the one thing she didn't want to talk about. A crash-and-burn love life wasn't on her list of hot topics. But when her friend asked her how things were going between her and Drew, she had no choice but to tell the truth.

The two women sat in a small booth tucked into the corner of a local steak house for a late dinner and lots of wine. Most of the action had moved to the bar area, so they had the dining room mainly to themselves.

"He has a wife," she finally said, spinning her wine glass by its stem. It still pissed her off to say it, even though that wasn't the worst of it. "Not only does he have a wife," she said, "he has a pregnant wife... and a two-year-old son."

Julia, her best friend and confidant, sat back, her wine glass empty, and stared at Sage with unblinking eyes. "No," she said. "There's no way..."

Sage chuckled but the bitterness burned. "Oh, trust me. There's a way. Because I met her."

Julia's hand flew to cover her wide-open mouth. Then in a half whisper, she said, "No way, that is messed up. What a complete dick. Seriously, what a total friggin' jerk."

Several weeks back, not realizing Sage would be there, Drew and his wife were on a date night which included the gallery show where Sage had been selling prints of her photographs. When a lovely woman wanted to buy a print for her son's room, she'd brought her husband to look at it. Rather than look at and be impressed by the photo, he looked like the proverbial deer caught in the headlights as Sage had smiled at him with murder in her eyes and a silent break splitting her heart.

"Did you say anything to the wife?" Julia asked. "I think I would have said something. At least enough to make her suspicious of her husband's assholery."

"I thought about it," she admitted with a laugh at Julia's word choice. "But it just didn't feel right." She sipped from her water glass as the waiter slipped their empty plates off the table. "It was so odd, Jules. Like, I felt bad hurting her feelings. She was so nice to me. It's like I wanted to tell her because it's not her fault she married a jackass. Still, I didn't feel like it was my place to ruin her marriage." She shrugged, looked to Julia for confirmation. "Does that make sense?"

Julia nodded. "Yeah, it does." She smiled and the simple gesture soothed Sage's agitation. "So, what happens now? You're not seeing him anymore, right?"

"God, no. Six weeks of Drew Davison was enough to last multiple lifetimes." Resting her face in her hands, she sighed. "I have no idea what's next. I'm thinking there must be a convent somewhere nearby I can join."

"I think that ship might have sailed, my friend," Julia said, eyeing Sage with a healthy dose of skepticism. Reaching over, she playfully shook Sage's arm. "Come on. Don't give up. There is a guy out there for you, I promise."

"Ugh, I think *that* ship has sailed." Sage took a long drink of water to help clear some of the Cabernet from her brain. She was tired of finding a guy, thinking he could be 'the one' and then learning the reason why he was still single. Or in Drew's case, just a total dick.

None of them had been long-term boyfriends but it still hurt when 'what could have been' turned into 'what never will be.' The one thing she certainly didn't want to think about was the one commonality between all of those failed relationships: Sage, herself.

"OK, my real estate agent friend, I need your advice," Sage said.

"With what, my heartbroken friend? Need me to find you a house somewhere with a better class of guys?"

"You half got it," Sage said.

"I don't understand." Julia leaned forward, searched Sage's face. "You want me to buy you a house or you want me to find you a better class of guys?"

Before she could change her mind, she blurted it out. "I've been thinking of moving." There. She said it. It was out in the open now and not just an idea bouncing around her brain, which, somehow, made it feel more real.

"Moving?" Julia said, sitting bolt upright. "As in packing up your life and leaving Boston? By yourself?"

Sage laughed at Julia's shocked look. "You do realize I'm an adult, right? I'm pretty sure by the time my parents were thirty-six, they were married, had a house, and I was in school."

"Yes, of course I know you're an adult, but why would you move? It's not like you'll be running into Drew and his wife all over town."

Julia was right, but it didn't dim the spark to try something new. "It's more than Drew and his wife. It's the whole string of them." She ticked off fingers as she counted the number of guys she'd dated recently. "Six, Jules. Six of them. They all turned out to be just as terrible as the last." She dropped her hands to the table, her heart heavy. "And that's just in the past year and a half."

Depressed all over again, she reached for her wine glass, but Julia moved it and slid her water glass in front of her instead. "You still have to get home tonight." She grinned and said, "But let me think about this whole moving thing for a minute."

"Why do *you* need to think about whether *I* should move or not?" Sage asked.

"Because you're my best friend and I can't just sit idly by while you run away and toss your career to the curb because some guy was a douche."

"I'm not running away," Sage said, defensive about her friend questioning her motives. "From Drew or anyone else. I'm just looking for something different. A change of scenery for a little while." She shrugged. "I just need to get out of Boston. Who knows? Maybe finding new things to photograph will be just what the doctor ordered. Besides, it was six guys who turned out to be douches."

After being quiet for several seconds, her brows knitted together in a pensive look. Julia slapped her hands down onto the table, rattling the silverware and stunning Sage. "I know," she said. "What about a vacation home?"

Curious, Sage waited for her to finish her thought.

"Don't just sell your place and leave town. Your life is here. That would be stupid." Julia grinned again, showing off those perfectly straight, perfectly white teeth. "What about looking at a vacation place somewhere? You could look up in New Hampshire or Maine. Really anywhere in New England and still be able to drive there in a few hours." She gripped her hands into excited little fists then yanked her bag from the seat next to her and rifled through it to get to her phone.

At first blush the idea of a vacation place held promise. A place she could go without telling anyone—that would be key—and relax and work on her photography. A change of pace when she needed it, but still with the surety of home.

"Here!" Julia yelled. She shoved the phone in front of Sage's face. "Something like this."

Sage focused on the thumbnail photo of a real-life gingerbread cottage. "Where is this?" she asked, easily imagining herself on a wicker chair on the front porch, sipping her morning coffee, wrapped in a comfy throw. "This is adorable."

Julia beamed across the table. "Right? See what I mean? That place is out in the Berkshires. I know a woman who lives part-time out there and she freaking loves it. It would take you a little more than two hours to be there from right here." She poked her finger into the tabletop for emphasis. "And the best part is that you could totally buy that place and still be rich."

"And let me guess," Sage said with a laugh. "There are enough bedrooms to be able to invite my best friend to stay with me from time to time?"

Thinking of her own little hideaway, even if it did include Julia occasionally, brought a thrill to Sage's heart. She had been out to the Berkshires a few times growing up. The green hills and abundance of space held a considerable appeal when contrasted with the hustle and noisy crowds of city life. But, with the incredible atmosphere of the art scene and the world-class restaurants, she would still feel completely in her element.

Julia took the phone back, scrolled through and said, "Yep. Three bedrooms. Totally enough for yours truly to come hang out for a weekend or two." She scrolled around and clicked somewhere, frowned slightly, then put the phone down directly in front of Sage. "With a price like that, I think we might have to assume it needs some work though." Having a best friend who was a real estate agent had its benefits. "This place was only listed today. I can contact the listing agent and see if we—" Julia put her hand over her heart, eyes pleading with Sage. "Assuming you want me, that is—"

"Wouldn't do it without you, Jules."

"Yay," Julia squeaked. "I'll contact them and see if we can take a look over the weekend."

"Or you can just put in an offer and see what happens," Sage blurted out.

"You're not serious," Julia said.

The music pumping out of the bar area on the far side of the dining room mingled with the sounds of happy people enjoying their lives, and it all sent a thrill of excitement through her. "Yeah," Sage said. "You know what? I am serious. Let's do this."

For the first time all evening Julia was silent. Sage worried her friend had thought she'd gone off the deep end, until a slow smile crept across Julia's face. Sage knew that look. An idea was brewing. "Yes," Julia said. "This is going to be amazing."

"What is?"

"This," she said, pointing at the image of the house on the phone. "You buy the place, sight unseen, and it's an investment. You bring your camera and your equipment, and you document the whole thing." Julia's voice grew louder, her words faster. "You have a ton of people that follow you on the socials. You can totally put the whole thing online. Before, during, and after pictures. Photograph the people you get to come in and do the stuff you can't. I love watching all those house flipping shows, but those are professionals. Show us all what it looks like when an average person tries to do it."

"Like a one-woman fixer upper show," Sage mused. "I've never done anything like that. I don't even know how to do anything like that. Am I crazy for wanting to try this? Or for thinking this sounds like a wicked lot of fun? I am, right? I'm out of my mind," she said. All at once, she didn't care if she was. "Let's do it. Put in the offer and see where it goes. What's the worst that could happen, right?"

"Right," Julia said. "Give it a few months and if it doesn't work out, put the place back on the market, no harm, no foul." She sat back again, exhausted by her own excitement.

The women clinked their water glasses in a toast, and as the waiter returned Sage slid her credit card for him to take.

"No, wait," Julia protested. "This is supposed to be on me, remember? I took you out to cheer you up."

Sage smiled. "You get me that house and we'll call it even."

Rowan

Five-year-olds playing tee-ball was the funniest shit Rowan Kennedy had seen all week. Aside from their short attention spans, these kids asked about a million questions and kept their coaches on their toes. Surrounded by intently watching eyes, Marcus had to field question after question that had nothing to do with tee-ball. *"Do you have a dog?" "How many kids do you have?" "What's your wife's name?" "Look, Coach Marcus... My shoes light up when I jump up and down."* And on and on. Rowan's own five-year-old spent most of the hour drawing in the dirt of the first base line with a stick, occasionally looking up and giving him a quick wave and a smile.

Now that practice had finished up for the morning, some of the kids wanted to play on the playground opposite the ball field, taking advantage of the warm spring day. "Can I go too, Dad?" Maisie asked as Rowan finger brushed her hair into a new ponytail and secured it with an elastic.

"Absolutely. Have fun," he said as she raced over to her friends.

A few kids had managed to convince their parents to let them stay, including one little boy whose mother had had a crush on Rowan pretty much since the day they met at kindergarten orientation in September. As she followed her son to the playground, Erica Becker gave Rowan a coy smile and then sashayed—there was no other word for it—across the parking lot, turning back when she got there to make sure he had watched.

Pulling his baseball cap lower over his eyes, he turned toward his oldest friend. Marcus stood beside him, watching the whirling balls of energy running and jumping and sliding all over the playground.

"I don't know if I'm cut out for this, dude. I have never seen energy levels like that," Marcus said, scrubbing a hand through his hair. "Look at them. They're still going strong and I'm ready for a goddamn nap." He laughed, shook his head. "I don't know how you live like that. Every. Single. Day."

"Honestly, you get used to it," Rowan said. "And you start looking forward to bedtime as soon as dinner's done."

"If you say so." Marcus lifted the batting tee and the bag of balls into the back of his Jeep. "Hey, I talked to your mom the other day when I was down at the Grind. She said Nick's house should be coming up for sale soon."

Rowan's mother, Delores, worked the mid-morning shift at the local diner, The Daily Grind, and she knew everything that happened in the small, Berkshire Mountain town of Hazelton. She wasn't a gossip, but she did love to talk.

"That's what his daughter said," Rowan replied. "She's got him all moved into an in-law apartment they built for him and they're selling his place pretty much as is."

For the past three years Rowan and Maisie had been living with Delores in her big farmhouse, saving money and waiting for Nick's house to come up for sale. It was a small three bedroom down the street from Delores, with a small front yard and a large open lot behind it. It was perfect for what he and Maisie needed and was still close enough to his mother, who cared for Maisie after school.

"Nice. It shouldn't need too much work before you move in?" Marcus leaned against the back of his Jeep, dark sunglasses covering his eyes.

"It needs a shit ton of updating, cosmetic stuff, but nothing structural that I could tell. Pretty much all the wiring needs to be updated though, the bathrooms need to be gutted and brought into the twenty-first century," Rowan said. "And those fucking carpets have to go. Nothing I can't handle with a few weeks of work and hopefully a good plumber to help me out?" Rowan raised his eyes to Marcus's. They had worked on more than one renovation together, including their current job at a local inn, and aside from being his best friend, Marcus did impeccable work.

"Absolutely, man. You know that. What do you have in there now, a full and a half bath?"

"Yeah. There's a decent sized half bath off the kitchen and then the master bath off the main bedroom. There's only the two bedrooms upstairs, no bathrooms, so I'm going to need a tub installed in the half bath downstairs so the kid's not always in my room."

Marcus nodded. "What are you looking at for the master bath? A whirlpool tub with enough room for a guest?" His face never moved but behind the glasses Rowan knew Marcus was needling him.

"You too?"

"Don't know what you're talking about." Marcus's lip quirked up before he schooled it back to neutral.

"God, how much time did you spend talking with my mother? She's got you trying to hook me up with some female now, too?"

Rowan said. "I'll tell you what I told her, I am all set with women right now. Once Maisie is grown up and out of the house, I'll revisit my plans. But right now, single life is my life."

Marcus shrugged one shoulder. "Dude, swear to God, I was just thinking about resale value. Issues much?" He grinned. "But seriously, what about Erica over there? She's easy to look at and she clearly wants you."

"Sin-gle," Rowan said slowly, for emphasis. "I want. To stay. Single." His phone rang in his pocket, and he was glad for the distraction from the uncomfortable topic of the woman who kept staring at him. "Hey, Ma, what's up?" he said, answering the call. "Maisie and I are at the playground."

She didn't even say hello but jumped into the conversation with both feet. "Honey, I just got off the phone with Sarah. You know, Nick's daughter?"

"Cool. Is the house finally hitting the market?" Rowan's heart lifted. He'd been patient for the past three years and now it was down to the formalities. "I just have to put the call in to my real estate agent and we should be good to go."

His mother hesitated, took a quick breath before she spit out, "Honey, the house is already sold."

The phone slipped from his hand, but he fumbled to catch it before it hit the ground. He held it back to his ear as his mother finished saying, "...too good to pass up."

Marcus stepped toward him. "Everything OK?" he asked.

Rowan shook his head to Marcus then, not believing what he heard, said to his mother, "Wait. Say that again."

"Sarah said that someone really wanted the place, and they offered her way above asking price. Now that she is taking care of her dad, the extra money will really be helpful for them." Delores sighed. "Rowan, honey, I am so sorry. But don't worry. We'll figure something out."

He ended the call with his mother and looked at Marcus. "They sold the house," he said, his heart dropping into his shoes. "They sold the fucking house to someone else." The feeling of hurt and betrayal was worse than the disappointment at not getting the place. Years of daydreaming and planning and working and saving just flew out the window and there wasn't a single thing he could do about it. His stomach physically ached from a metaphorical sucker punch.

"Shit," Marcus said. "I'm sorry, man. What happened?"

As he repeated the little information he had gotten from his mother, the words tasted like poison in his mouth. "Someone bought my house right out from under me," he said. "I'm gonna be stuck living at my mother's house forever. How the fuck did that even happen?"

"Daddy!" Maisie's voice broke into the conversation. "That's a swear word. Gramma says you can't say that word. It's not nice."

Rowan reached down and scooped his daughter into his arms. "You're right, Zee. That is a bad word. I'll put some dollars in the jar, and I won't say it again."

With her requisite flair, Maisie rolled her eyes and said, "Yeah, right," and broke into giggles when Rowan tickled her ribs.

"All done playing?" he asked her.

"Yup. I'm hungry and Noah was being mean to me," she said.

"Who's Noah?" Rowan asked.

Marcus nudged his arm, quietly said, "Erica's kid," and nodded in her general direction.

"Oh, Christ."

"Daddy!"

"Sorry, sorry. I'll put an extra dollar in the jar."

Scrubbing a hand over his face to try to wipe away the shock of the phone call without letting on that he was upset, Rowan looked from Maisie to Marcus, who smiled and clapped him on the shoulder. "Let me know if you need anything, alright?" Marcus said. "You'll figure it out, man. Don't stress." Rowan nodded as Marcus reached over to tap Maisie on the nose. "Good job today, kiddo. You're a natural out there."

"Thanks, Uncle Marcus," she said, and rested her head on Rowan's shoulder. The weight of her in his arms grounded Rowan in the moment. Relief washed over him as he realized that since he'd never told her about wanting the house, she couldn't be disappointed about not getting it.

Probably the only saving grace of the day.

Sage

S age Lowery stood in the god-awful living room of her new vacation home. Her best friend and real estate agent extraordinaire, Julia, had come out to help her get settled and after a weekend of wine, takeout pizza, driving around town, and sleeping on blow up mattresses, Julia had gone back to Boston with a promise to follow Sage's social updates and another promise to come back for a visit in a few weeks.

Tackling the renovations of the little gingerbread cottage in the Berkshires was Sage's way of stepping out of, and hopefully hitting the reset button on, her life. Leaving her apartment and temporarily relocating to Hazelton would be completely new and unfamiliar enough to keep her mind occupied with thoughts other than her dead-end love life.

Her original vision of being married, and maybe even having a child, was nowhere on the horizon, and showed no promise of being there anytime soon. Certainly not with the string of 'bums,' as her grandfather used to call anyone who didn't meet his standards, she'd been dating.

Julia's grand plan was for Sage, as a professional photographer, to document her adventure on her popular social media accounts, thereby keeping her name in front of potential clients while she spent the next several months in the beautifully scenic western end of Massachusetts.

She and Julia had come up with a master to-do list and Sage was determined to make even minimal progress on her first full day alone. The inside of the house needed the most work, but the early June morning was already warm, so once Julia pulled out of the driveway, Sage grabbed her camera and tripod and headed out to tackle the first step of her renovations: the *before* pictures.

The small flower beds along the front porch were full of color. There were white and yellow flowers and purple ones that added a nice pop of color to the yard, though aside from the daisies, she had no idea what they were called. Looking from her new garden up to the porch, she knew the first thing to do would be to get a chair and a small table so she could sit out there and read with a glass of water, or wine, after a hard day's work. She pulled out her phone and typed 'table and chair—front porch' into her already sizable list.

After looking back at the unknown flowers, she quickly added 'research flowers in front yard.'

"Good morning," said a soft female voice from behind her.

Sage's new home sat halfway down Orchard Street, an adorable neighborhood of smaller homes with deep green grass and brightly colored gardens similar to her own. Looking up, she saw an older woman smiling at her from the sidewalk. The woman stood beside a little girl, with a gigantic pink helmet, sitting astride a pink bicycle with white, plastic training wheels.

She hadn't heard them approach, but it was still nice that they stopped to say hello. "Morning," Sage responded, assuming they would keep going on their walk. When they didn't move, she stepped closer to them, stuck her hand out to shake. "My name's Sage," she said. "I just moved here."

"Delores," the woman said. "And this is my granddaughter, Maisie."

"I'm five," the little cyclist said with a grin and held up her hand with all her fingers splayed. "I'm learning to ride my bike," she added.

"That's exciting," Sage said. "It's a lovely bike. It matches your helmet."

"And my shoes," she said, kicking one foot up in the air.

Delores smiled down on her granddaughter, her affection for the girl obvious.

"Do you both live around here?" Sage asked.

"We do," Delores said, pointing over her shoulder to a large white house on the opposite side of the street, a few houses away.

Sage had noticed the house while she and Julia were exploring the new neighborhood because it was larger and of a different style than the rest.

"We live over there. We were friends with Nick," Delores said, looking at Sage, clearly expecting that she would know who Nick was. "The man who used to own this house," Delores finally said when Sage didn't respond.

"Oh," she said. "Sorry. I dealt with a woman named Sarah. I didn't realize someone else lived here."

"Sarah is Nick's daughter. He is getting up there in age and Sarah thought it would be better for him to live with her and her husband," Delores explained.

"Mr. Nick was my friend," Maisie added. "I helped him plant flowers."

"Well, that was very nice of you," Sage said. "Mr. Nick was lucky to have such a nice friend to help him. I'll bet he misses you."

"He does," Maisie said in such a matter-of-fact tone that Sage and Delores both chuckled at her confidence. "Are you taking pictures?" Maisie asked, pointing to the camera hung around Sage's neck.

"I am, yes," Sage said. "I'm a photographer and I'm going to be taking pictures of the house and the yard the way it all looks today. Then I'll be taking more pictures as I fix things up and then I'll take some more when the work is all done." She looked at Delores. "I sort of bought the house on a whim and figured I'd have a little fun with it while I fix it up."

Delores smiled at her, but the smile didn't quite reach her eyes. "That sounds fun," she said. "Do you plan to keep it once it's done or are you going to flip it?"

"Haven't really planned that far out to be honest with you. I've given myself until Labor Day to make that decision. I've never lived outside of Boston before and I'm not sure if I can do it." She laughed. "But I needed a change of scenery and—" she raised her arms out to her sides, encompassing her new home and yard, "this part of the state is so beautiful. Besides, if home ownership doesn't work out for me, I can flip the house, like you said, and go back to Boston."

"Very sensible," Delores said.

The desire to get back to her task conflicted with the pressure to keep making small talk with her new neighbors. Just as she was about to thank them for stopping by, Maisie said, "I like those flowers." She looked up at Sage, her round eyes full of expectation. "They're really pretty."

The bright flowers brought life to the front of her new house. Was she ready to let this little girl have them, to take the few bits of color from her garden? The bigger question was whether she was willing to let herself become part of the life of this new town, or should she let them go on their way and stay closed off in her own little world?

"Would you like to take some home with you?" Sage finally asked.

Stopping long enough to get the nod of approval from her grandmother, the little girl hopped off her bike and ran full speed into Sage's yard.

Sage made eye contact with Delores then held up her camera. "Do you mind if I take a few while she picks? I can send them to you if you give me your info."

Delores smiled, this time the gesture felt much more genuine. "Why not?"

Maisie stood stock still in front of the flowers, her hands clasped together behind her back, staring at them as if they were made of glass. Quickly focusing, Sage snapped a few shots of her, still wearing her giant bike helmet, which gave the skinny girl the appearance of a quilting pin.

"Why don't you pick out your five favorite flowers," Sage suggested. "I just have to run inside and grab a few things." A couple minutes later she returned with a stack of wet paper towels, a square of aluminum foil and a pair of scissors. "Did you pick the ones you want?"

Maisie nodded. "Uh huh. I want these," she said, pointing to a section of all yellow flowers.

"You like yellow?" Sage asked.

"It's my favorite color," Maisie said, then frowned. "I want to paint my room yellow, but my dad won't let me."

Sage looked to Delores who crinkled her nose as she smiled, an endearing gesture. "My son isn't exactly a morning person and Maisie's room faces due east."

Sage smiled at Maisie, "Maybe someday," she said. "OK, what do you say we get this bouquet put together?"

Maisie nodded.

Carefully, Sage handed her the scissors. "You cut the flowers you want, and I'll hold them until you're done."

Maisie's eyes went wide as she held the big scissors in her hand, then her brows drew in, her expression turned serious. She cut each flower, handing them to Sage in turn. When she was done, Sage had her cut a few pieces of greenery from some nearby plants to fill out the bouquet.

While Sage held the bundle in her hand, she said to Maisie, "Now you want to wrap up these stems with the paper towels." Maisie did. "And now wrap the foil around the bottom and up the stems to keep the towels from dripping water until you get home and can put them in a vase, OK?"

Maisie's face beamed as she raced with her flowers back to her grandmother's side. "Look what I made for Daddy!"

"He's going to love it," Delores said, taking the bouquet from Maisie so she could hop back onto her bike. "Should we go home and put these in some water?"

"Yup!"

"All right," Delores said, "But what do you say to Miss Sage first?"

Maisie jumped off her bike again and sprinted toward Sage, threw her arms around her midsection. "Thank you for helping me make the flowers, Miss Sage."

Sage's interactions with small children were few and far between and the little girl's easy affection was sweet but still awkward. She patted Maisie's back. "You're very welcome."

Maisie raced back and climbed onto her bike. "Can I come over to your house again?"

Was there some kind of etiquette rule about letting neighborhood children into your home? This wasn't something Sage had ever dealt with in the city. She didn't know whether to say yes and have Delores think she was some kind of creep or say no and have her think she was some kind of jerk with no social skills.

Delores came to her rescue when she said, "Maisie, it's not polite to invite yourself over to someone else's house, sweetheart." She looked back at Sage. "But that doesn't mean we can't invite Miss Sage over to our house."

"Yay! Do you want to come to our house?" Maisie said.

"Well, I can't today, but some other time would be lovely. Thank you for asking."

"I don't know if you've been down Main Street at all yet," Delores said. "But if you'd ever like to come in for a cup of coffee and the best blueberry muffins around, I work the ten to two shift at The Daily Grind during the week while Maisie's in school. Of course, you're always welcome to come by the house too. It was nice to meet you, Miss Sage."

As Delores and Maisie slowly made their way toward their house, sunlight glinting off the spokes of Maisie's tires, Sage turned her attention back to her photos. Half an hour later she had dozens of shots of her house from all angles, along with the landscaping, and several more of the neighborhood in general.

Satisfied with what she had to work with, she clicked the lens cap back in place and went up the front steps to sit on the porch and relax before going inside to start taking photos in there. Leaning back on her hands with her legs outstretched, she sank into the peace of the late morning.

Bright sunshine bathed her skin as a black pickup truck rolled down the street. It slowed noticeably as it neared her house but then picked up speed again as she squinted to get a better look at the driver.

Unnerved by that bit of weirdness, Sage hauled herself to her feet and went inside.

Sage

By the middle of the week, she had made significant progress on her list, mostly cosmetic things, but they made a difference. The ugly carpets in the two bedrooms on the second floor had been torn out and the plastic-coated wire shelving had been removed from the walls of one of the rooms. Clearly the previous owner had been using the room as a giant closet.

Getting the carpets down the stairs by herself was messy, dirty work, and she'd had to cut them into smaller strips and carry them piece by piece to the small dumpster sitting in her driveway. The shelving was in decent shape, and she stacked it along one wall in case she was able to reuse some of it inside the actual closets.

Thursday dawned warm and bright, and she'd spent the first half of the morning taking photos and uploading them with a bit of narration to her social feeds. After her stomach growled painfully one too many times, she decided to take up the invitation from her new neighbor and head down to the coffee shop to see about those blueberry muffins.

Delores caught her eye as soon as she entered The Daily Grind, waving her over to a stool about halfway down the counter. Passing by two men with broad backs, she paused momentarily to enjoy the view, before reminding herself that she was out in the Berkshires to get away from guys, not just find different ones.

Delores grinned knowingly when she caught Sage looking. "Sage, honey, you just have a seat and I'll grab you a coffee."

"Thanks, Delores."

Trying her best to ignore the men beside her, she grabbed a menu and looked over her options. As hard as she tried, though, the feeling of being watched led her to put down the menu and glance to her left. Quickly, the guy closest to her turned his head forward again, but not before catching her eye. His face was handsome enough but didn't hold a speck of friendliness.

A smiling Delores appeared in front of her with a steaming cup of coffee. Just as she was about to take Sage's order, the door opened, and an elderly couple shuffled through. "Let me just go help them to a table. I'll be back in a flash," Delores said, then rolled her eyes playfully and said, "Well, maybe not a flash, but I'll be back in a minute."

Looking for some cream for her coffee, the nearest set was in front of the grumpy dude. Leaning slightly in his direction she reached for them. "Excuse me, can I just grab the—"

Without turning his head or saying a word, his arm flew out, grabbed the caddy, and slid it down the counter with a little too much force.

Catching it before it flew by her, she said, "Uh... thanks?"

"Dude," his friend said quietly, nudging him with his elbow. "What the fuck?"

Asshole, because that's how Sage referred to him now, turned his head slightly, mumbled, "Welcome," and went back to drinking his coffee, staring straight ahead, while Sage grabbed a couple creamers from the silver holder.

"Here you go, honey," Delores said, suddenly there, pouring an unnecessary refill of Sage's coffee. Delores must have seen the way Asshole behaved because she narrowed her eyes at him, before turning back to Sage, filled with nothing but sunshine. "Can I get you one of those blueberry muffins I told you about or are you looking for something a little more filling today?"

"Thank you," Sage said as she peeled the top of a creamer, stirred it into her coffee. "I think I'll just stick with the muffin today, thanks, Delores."

"Good choice," she said. "Be back in a snap."

Chancing a look at Asshole, though she had no idea why, he had turned to talk with his friend and seemed to have forgotten that Sage was there. It was unfortunate that he had to be such a jerk, because he was awfully nice to look at. She had always had a thing for arms and boy did this guy have them. Dark jeans hugged his strong thighs, and the work boots only added to the sexiness. *Nice choice, Sage. Way to be attracted to the worst guy in the room.*

When Delores returned with Sage's blueberry muffin, Asshole attempted to stop her for another refill on his coffee.

"You can wait your turn," Delores said as she fixed him with another look, then set the plate in front of Sage. "Can I get you anything else, honey? More coffee?"

Sage bit the inside of her cheeks to keep from laughing out loud as Delores fussed over her, much to Asshole's displeasure. Too damn bad, maybe he should be less of a jerk.

He sucked in an audible breath and sighed it out as he stood and opened his wallet. "Never mind the coffee," he said, tucking a few bills beneath his plate. "I've gotta get back to work." Slapping his friend on the shoulder, he said, "See you in a few."

Once he was out the door, Sage whispered to Delores because she didn't want his friend to overhear, in case he was a big jerk too. "Delores, what was that all about?"

"What was what all about?"

Sage wasn't sure if Delores truly didn't know or if she was being obtuse on purpose. "That man that just left. Why did I get the feeling he wanted to stab me with his butter knife?"

Delores threw her head back and laughed. "Oh, don't worry about him. He's all bluster, that one. You just eat up and give me a yell when you're ready for more coffee." With that she hurried away to welcome another older couple that had walked through the door.

Since the jerk had gone, the tension in the room had gone to zero and Sage managed to enjoy her late breakfast. "Thank you so much," she said to Delores as she left a ten-dollar bill under her coffee cup. "That muffin was even better than you promised it would be."

"Glad to hear it," Delores said. "Come back any time."

Sage was just about out the door when she remembered there was something she'd meant to ask. "Oh," she said, turning back around. "I know I could just search it online, but sometimes it's better to ask people who know the area. I need an electrician to do some work on the house before I can begin to do some of the bigger stuff. Do you know of a good electrician around here?"

The man that sat at the counter looked up at Delores and some kind of unspoken communication passed between them. Delores frowned at him then reached into her apron pocket, pulled out a slip of paper. "Of course, I do." She scribbled something on the paper and handed it to the man. "Give this to her, will you, Marcus?"

Marcus held Delores's gaze a beat too long then spun the stool around and stood to give Sage the paper. His tall frame filled up the space, but his demeanor was not at all off-putting. "He's really good at what he does. The best around." Marcus smiled at her, and she noted how different he was from Asshole-guy. "Just shoot him a text and he'll get right back to you."

Sage looked from Delores to Marcus to the paper in her hands. A phone number had been written under the name Rowan Kennedy.

Rowan

Rowan, Maisie, and Delores had finished an early dinner, and Rowan was trying to get his daughter ready for tee-ball practice while he also helped his mother clear the dinner dishes. "Come on, Zee," he said. "Run upstairs and put on your clothes for practice." He took the dishes from his mother's hand as she rinsed them then he loaded them into the dishwasher. "You know you're not supposed to rinse these first. That's the whole point of the dishwasher."

Maisie didn't leave the kitchen, instead stood in the doorway, her face set in a frown. "But I don't know what are clothes for practice and what aren't."

"I left out some shorts and a tee shirt on the end of your bed, Maisie," Delores said over her shoulder. "Run up and put them on, OK?"

"'K," Maisie said as she took off at a run.

"I gave the new neighbor your phone number after you left the diner this morning."

"What for?" he said, his shoulders immediately tight. His feelings about her were fairly obvious, he thought, and his feelings on her buying Nick's house were more obvious than that. It made no difference that she was gorgeous, a fact he tried all day to forget; she was the enemy.

"Because she's lonely and she's looking for a date," Delores said, then smacked his shoulder like he was a fly she was trying to squash. "She just bought a house that needs electrical work," she said, irritation dripping from each word. "And you know...you being an electrician and all."

Rubbing his sore shoulder, he asked, "So, you just randomly said, 'Hey, my son's an electrician, you should call him so he can die on the inside while he does work on your house that should be his.'? And she was like, 'That's great. Let me call and make his fucking life more miserable than it already is.'"

Under most circumstances, Delores Kennedy had the patience of a saint. This wasn't most circumstances. "Are you serious right now?" she asked, her eyes narrowing and her lips pressing into a thin line. "The woman asked if I knew an electrician. My son happens to be the best electrician around. What was I supposed to do, Rowan? Give her Joe Kemp's number? Or lie and tell her I don't know anyone?"

Her voice grew louder as she continued, her unblinking eyes pinning him in place. "Look," she said. "I know you don't like living here. I understand that. I know you were looking forward to being able to buy Nick's place so you can get out of here. But it didn't happen that way. And you know what? That's just too damn bad. Life doesn't always go the way we want it to." She shoved another dish into his hands. "You didn't want Jess to leave either."

"I don't want to talk about Jess," he cut in.

"I know you don't, but at some point, you're going to have to talk about her," Delores said. "You didn't want her to leave, and you certainly didn't want to be a single parent. Nobody blames you for that. But you have a choice to make. You can keep wallowing in self-pity and be angry at the woman who moved in across the street. Or you can put on your big boy pants and be the professional that you are and help her. She is a customer, Rowan. You don't have to be her best friend. Do the job. Get paid. Put the money toward a different house."

By the time she finished laying into him her face was red and the dish clutched in her hand was half a second from shattering into pieces from the pressure of her grip. She turned back to the sink and rinsed the dish for a few seconds. "I'm sorry living here and having me take care of your daughter makes your life so miserable."

Fuck. He'd hurt her feelings. The tension in his shoulders crept into his neck and he tilted his head side to side to work out the stress. "Ma, that's not what I meant. It's not miserable living here. I... I just really wanted a place of my own, you know? I'm thirty-seven years old and having to move back home was never on my list of life goals."

He stood by her side and wrapped an arm around her shoulders, pulled her in with a squeeze. "I couldn't have made it the last three years without you, and you know it." He leaned over and planted a small kiss on the top of her head. "But I don't think I can do it. I can't go over to that house and do work for some other owner." Even if she was hot as hell. "What the fuck was Sarah thinking when she didn't even tell me she had that other offer?"

Delores turned on him. "You leave Sarah out of this. Building that in-law apartment and taking Nick to live with them was not cheap, Rowan. She needed all the money she could get. The woman, her name is Sage, by the way, offered Sarah way over asking price. What was she supposed to say? No?"

"She could have given me a fucking chance to match it," Rowan said as he shoved the top dishwasher rack back in place and slammed the door shut.

"Daddy, that's two dollars you have to put in the jar!" Dressed in her practice clothes, Maisie skipped into the room, her blue eyes large and round. She stopped by his side with one hand on her hip and the other held out for the money she knew was coming.

The swear jar had been Delores's idea after Maisie had gotten in trouble at school for repeating some of Rowan's more colorful language. Maisie loved it because she got to choose where to spend the money once the jar was full.

Reaching into his back pocket Rowan pulled out his wallet, flipped through and pulled out a five-dollar bill. "Here," he said. "This should cover me for the rest of the day."

Maisie snatched the money from his hand and ran to the nook where her grandmother stored the swear jar. Climbing up the step stool and holding the jar under one arm, she used her free hand to work at the lid without success.

"Need help, baby girl?" Rowan asked.

"Yes, please." She handed him the jar.

"You go put your shoes on and I'll put the money in." He lifted her slight body off the step stool and planted her on the ground where she took off at a run to get her shoes. Rowan opened the jar, stuffed the bill inside, then, after making sure Maisie wasn't looking, stuffed in another five before he closed it back up and returned it to the shelf.

His mother watched him, and a small smile pulled at her lips. She stood with her back against the counter and her after dinner tea clutched in her hands.

"Alright, baby girl, let's get out of here," he said as he grabbed his keys and his ball cap from the hook by the door.

"Have fun at tee-ball, Maisie," Delores called from across the kitchen.

"Thanks, Gramma." Maisie bolted out the door in front of Rowan.

"Just talk to her," Delores said quietly to Rowan's back.

He looked over his shoulder, questioning her with a look.

"Sage," Delores said. "When she calls or texts or whatever. Just talk to her."

He knew that tone. Matchmaker Delores had joined the conversation. "Right. Because she's just a client, right, Ma? No need to be friends with the woman."

"She is very pretty, dear. But I just want you to talk to her about the electrical work she needs done. What else you talk about with her is entirely up to you." Delores grinned from behind her teacup. He swore her eyes twinkled.

"Bye, Ma."

Rowan

The drive from the house to the tee-ball field was less than five minutes, but that didn't save him from having to explain himself to his daughter.

"Daddy, how come you don't like Miss Sage?"

"I don't not like her, Zee."

"She's really pretty and she helped me pick flowers from her garden for you. Didn't you like them? I thought they were really pretty, and they smelled pretty, too."

His eyes flicked to the rear-view mirror where he held her gaze for a second before returning to the road. "They were beautiful, and that was really nice of Miss Sage to let you pick them." Not only was this woman beautiful to look at, but she had to be nice to his mother and his daughter, too? *Not fair, Universe.* He secretly wished Sage had been a bitch to one of them, so at least he'd have a valid excuse to pawn her off on Joe Kemp. "She was nice to you and Gramma, huh?"

"Uh huh," she said. "But Gramma said I couldn't invite myself to her house 'cos it isn't polite."

Rowan laughed.

"But then she said that we can invite Miss Sage to our house," she said.

The laughter died in Rowan's throat. "She said what? You invited her to the house? Why didn't Gramma say anything about that to me?"

"I dunno."

His fingers went cold as they gripped the steering wheel. Would she even say yes to the invitation? What if she didn't? What if she did? Would he have to be there? Would he want to be there?

"When is she coming over?" he asked.

"I dunno."

Pulling up to the field, Rowan saw other parents with little tee-ball players milling around the parking lot while they waited for the trio of coaches to bring the equipment over. Marcus carried a couple of tees and a bag of balls while one of the other coaches carried a mesh bag with helmets.

"When you talk to Miss Sage, can you invite her over? She might say yes to you," Maisie said.

"I don't think so, Zee. If I talk to Miss Sage, it will be to give her the number of another electrician." He pulled the truck to a stop in a parking spot next to the field.

"That's silly," she said, giggling.

He caught her eye in the rear view again. "Why is that silly?"

"'Cos you're a 'lectrician, Daddy."

He opened her door to let her down onto the pavement. "Freeze," he said when she turned to bolt to the field to be with her friends. Dutifully she came back and threw her arms around his waist for a quick hug. "OK," he said. "Now you can go." He picked her up and deposited her on the opposite side of the low wooden fence that separated the pavement from the green grass, and she ran down the small, sloping hill to join her team.

"She's so sweet," a sugary voice said from very close to him, startling him in the process. Erica Becker stood beside him, her long brown hair pulled into a high ponytail, large cat-like sunglasses hiding her eyes. Something about her dark red lips curling into a smile made her resemble the Grinch. "Is she enjoying tee-ball? Noah is having a blast with it."

"Oh, hey, Erica. Thanks, and yeah, I think she likes it well enough." He shrugged. "As much as a five-year-old likes anything, I guess." He looked down and saw Maisie and two other little girls playing a game of Ring Around the Rosie while Marcus tried lining up some of the other kids in rows behind the tees. One little boy held a bat and swung around in a complete circle, almost wiping out the line behind him, until one of the coaches made him stand still. He plopped unceremoniously to the ground and began wailing. Several other kids toward the back of the lines had congregated and began picking dandelions and chasing each other to throw the decapitated flowers at one another.

"Yikes," Erica said. "It's a bit of pandemonium down there, isn't it?"

With a laugh, Rowan agreed. The season was just about over, and the chaos was no less than it had been in April. "They're all first-time coaches and I think it might take a season or two to get the hang of dealing with little kids."

"Maybe you should have been the coach," Erica said, bumping her hip against his. "I'll bet you would be really good at being in charge. I know I would certainly do anything you asked."

Holy shit. Rowan was completely silent for fear of saying the wrong thing, and either offending her or encouraging her, unsure which would be worse.

The awkward silence appeared to be awkward only to him, as Erica stepped closer, giving him a nose-full of flowery perfume and an eyeful of cleavage as she crossed her arms and pushed her tits up, practically dumping them out of her tank top. *Subtle.*

Another mom approached them, and Erica dropped her arms to her sides, obviously not wanting to share the show with Amy Navarro. "Rowan. Erica," Amy said. "How are you guys?"

The women chatted with each other while Rowan took a step backward, hoping like hell to get away from Erica and using Amy's arrival to do so without seeming rude. Instead, Erica reached out and hooked her hand around his arm, pulled him back into the conversation.

"Rowan and I were just talking about how much fun the kids are having. How is Layla enjoying it so far?" Erica said.

As Amy was about to answer, Rowan's phone chimed. Unhooking Erica from his arm, he reached into his back pocket to check it. It was a text from an unknown number, but he knew right away who had texted him. "Pardon me, ladies." He held the phone up. "Never a day off, you know?" He checked one more time to make sure Maisie was doing alright then slid away from the women and walked across the gravel lot to Marcus's Jeep to give himself space.

Leaning his body against the hood, Rowan read the text.

> Hi! My name is Sage Lowery and I just moved to town and need some electrical work done. Delores at the coffee shop gave me your number! Any chance you have time to come by and give me an estimate? Thanks!

His instinct was to fire off a text listing everything he knew that needed to be done in that house. He knew all the outlets needed to be replaced, several dedicated lines needed to be installed, and several light switches needed to be replaced because Nick had somehow managed to break them. He knew all the plumbing that needed to be updated and replaced, the doors that stuck in the humid weather, and the windows that had broken locks and ripped screens. He knew what work had to be done to the floors and the walls to bring them into the modern age.

Holding the phone so tightly in his grip he feared the glass would crack, he typed up a reply.

> Sure. I can stop by Friday after I finish up my last job. 6:30 OK?

He would be home long before six-thirty, but he would need to see Maisie and make sure she had dinner and a bath before he left to go over to Nick's.

He had to stop thinking of it as Nick's place. It wasn't Nick's anymore. And it sure as shit wasn't his. He'd never even had the chance to put in a counteroffer and somehow the house had been sold out from under him. Fury burned through his veins, causing a prickle of sweat to break out along his hairline.

> 6:30 is perfect! 17 Orchard Street in Hazelton. See you then! Thank you!

She used too many exclamation points. Why did she use so many of the fucking things? A simple period would have gotten the message across without the unnecessary drama of all the fucking exclamation points.

Looking over to his truck, Amy and Erica were still there talking, so Rowan decided to spend the rest of the practice leaning against Marcus's Jeep with his phone out, hopefully giving the women the impression he was busy with work stuff.

The first thing he did was add Sage Lowery as a contact. If he was going to take her on as a client, he would certainly need to be able to text her. And if he didn't take her on as a client, he could delete her information. He scrubbed a hand through his hair as he imagined what it would be like going inside the house that should be his but wasn't.

The evening sun started to sink, and Rowan's spirit followed. Doom scrolling on his phone only made him feel worse, but the thought of Erica showing up next to him was enough to keep him mindlessly scrolling through screen after screen.

A quick time check showed about fifteen minutes left of Maisie's practice. Clicking open his browser, he pulled up a real estate site and input a few parameters to see if there was a house within a twenty-minute radius of Hazelton that was even remotely in his budget.

The first house on the list held some promise. He knew the neighborhood. It was in Hazelton, so Maisie wouldn't have to switch schools. From the outside it was nice, if a little dated, but nothing a coat of paint and some new landscaping couldn't fix. His stomach pinched when he saw the asking price. It was a touch over what he could afford, meaning he couldn't afford it at all. But it was close. Maybe another six months or so of squirreling away his money and a house like that could be theirs.

He looked at a few more homes, but nothing that would work for him and Maisie. At least not yet. Which meant when he met up with Sage Lowery, he had no choice but to take her on as a client. He needed the money and, already knowing what had to be done in the house, it would be easy money. Too easy to pass up. He just had to put on his game face and make it through to get the paycheck.

"Hey, buddy," Marcus said.

"I'm all done, Daddy," Maisie said, hopping up and down by Rowan's leg. "Can I go to the playground with Noah?"

Pushing himself up, Rowan lifted Maisie into his arms. "Sorry, Zee, not tonight. Maybe next time." She squirmed in his arms, trying to free herself to get to the playground. "Hey," he said, his tone clipped. "I said no. It's late and you need a tub before bed." She scowled and buried her face in his neck with a grunt but stopped trying to get free from his arms. To Marcus he said, "How'd it go out there? Finally getting the hang of it now that the season's almost over?" Rowan grinned at him, knowing full well he wasn't.

"Like herding cats," Marcus quipped. "Except for my girl here, right Maisie?" he said tickling under her chin until she giggled. Then he tossed the equipment into the back of the Jeep. "How's everything going with your neighbor? You talk to her yet?"

"I'm going over Friday after work to give her an estimate," Rowan said.

"So, you're gonna take the job then? Good for you, man," Marcus said. "I gotta tell you she seemed like a really nice person."

"She is a nice person," Maisie mumbled from Rowan's neck. "She's really pretty, too."

Marcus laughed, shrugged. "She's not wrong."

"'Night, Marcus," Rowan said as he carried Maisie back to the truck, away from his laughing friend. He turned around, taking a few backward steps. "If you think she's that pretty, I've got her number. Why don't you give her a call?"

"She's pretty cute. Maybe I will," Marcus said.

It shouldn't have pissed him off, but it did.

Sage

She looked around and admired her work as sweat poured down her back. Knees and elbows aching, fingertips ragged from all her hard work, Sage smiled. The plaster walls had been freed from the rose monstrosity wallpaper that had been covering them. The walls would need some basic repair and preparation before she painted them, but they were solid otherwise. The hardwood floors she'd revealed from beneath the shag carpeting were in a similar state to the walls; in need of some cleaning, but they didn't need to be replaced.

She'd gotten the occasional snarky comment and lots of spam comments as she posted her photos, but for the most part people were enjoying her content. Her followers weren't shy about sharing their dislike of the old décor and were quick to offer thoughts on colors and themes, some of which Sage took note of because they were good suggestions.

With forty minutes until the electrician was scheduled to show up, she had time to run the trash down to the dumpster, her belly screaming for food the whole time.

Looking at the clock on the stove, she decided she had time, and turned the oven on to preheat. In the master bathroom, she turned on the shower to warm up while she went back to the kitchen, opened a frozen pizza and tossed it in the oven.

The steamy heat of the shower eased her sore neck and back as she let the water stream over her aching body. The calming scent of lavender body wash reinforced her sense of ease and satisfaction at a day well spent. After toweling off, she threw on some loose sweatpants, her favorite Dropkick Murphys tee shirt, and tugged on an oversize hoodie. She brushed her long hair down her back to air dry, then threw on some fluffy Nordic slipper socks just as the timer buzzed from the kitchen.

Smelling the pizza as soon as she opened the bedroom door, she followed the scent like Hansel and Gretel and their trail of breadcrumbs. As she pulled her dinner from the oven, a knock sounded at the front door. She looked at the clock. He was ten minutes early. With a deep sigh and a longing look she slid the pizza onto a cutting board, tossed the oven mitt to the side.

Wondering how quickly she'd be able to get back to her dinner, she pulled the front door open. "Hi, thanks for..." Her words died on her tongue as she locked eyes with the same asshole guy from the diner. Clearly this was some kind of mistake. Why would Delores have given her this man's number? He obviously, but for reasons unknown, hated Sage. Even as he stood before her on her own front porch his look of disdain was unmistakable.

Quickly zipping her hoodie up a few more inches, she stepped onto the porch, forcing the man to take a step backward. He may be a wonderful electrician, but there was no way in hell she was letting him inside her house while she was home alone. Which would be always.

Sage recalled what Delores had told her at the diner, that he was all bluster, and hoped she was right. Closing the door, she said to him, "You must be Rowan." Extending her hand in greeting, she waited for him to respond. "I'm Sage Lowery. It's nice to meet you," she lied, when he didn't respond.

Finally, he shook her hand. "Rowan Kennedy," he said. "My mother told me you bought Nick's house."

His mother? Sage was firmly in the 'never let them see you sweat' category in her interactions with others, but she was sure Delores didn't tell her that. She lifted her lips into her sweetest smile. "Delores didn't mention you were her son."

"She's like that," he said, then looked over her shoulder and made the smallest movement to indicate he expected her to let him inside. When she didn't move or open the door for him, he huffed out a breath. "So, you wanna show me what you need done in there?"

Nope. Not happening. Everything about Rowan Kennedy gave off the dickhead vibe, which she found difficult to reconcile to the kind woman and sweet-as-sugar little girl she met last week. Yet, there they were in a standoff on her front porch. "You know, Rowan," she said, not trying to hide the edge in her voice. "I think maybe I'll be holding off on the electrical work for a while, so... sorry to make you come all the way over here for nothing, but I think I'm all set."

Anger flared behind his eyes, but she didn't give a crap about his anger or his dislike of her or whatever the hell the rest of his issues were. She wanted exactly two things at that moment. The first was a great big piece of pizza. The second was for Rowan Kennedy to get his angry ass the hell off her porch. When he didn't react right away, Sage said, "Good night," and turned to go back into her house.

"You don't want to put that work off," he said as she reached for the doorknob.

She turned to face him. "And why is that?" Why she was continuing this conversation was beyond her at that moment. Maybe she wanted to see if she could get some kind of response from him that wasn't hostile. Or maybe it was the way the muscle in his jaw kept tweaking and she liked poking the bear.

"Well, if you'd like to run a microwave in the kitchen while you're using a hair dryer in the bathroom on the other side of the wall, or if you want to put AC units in any of the bedroom windows because summer is hot out here. Or, you know, if you want to plug anything into any of the outlets on the first floor without the cords always falling out of the loose sockets. Or any number of reasons I would be happy to explain to you."

She had a difficult time imagining him happy to do anything.

He took a small step back from her before he said, "Look, I've been inside this house a million times with Nick. I am well aware of the work that needs to be done in there. But if you'd be more comfortable hiring another electrician, fine by me. But just get someone in here before you start doing too many renovations that you'll only have to re-do after the electrical work is all done."

The entire time he spoke his face never changed. He never smiled or showed any sign of being nice, but the things he said made sense. She looked him in the eye for an extended moment. He had Delores's eyes but aside from that he must have favored his father. Poor Delores, she thought, having to put up with two men like that.

She took a step toward him, putting them just as close as they had been a minute ago. Her curiosity had gotten the better of her. "Did I do something wrong?" she asked, still looking up into his hard eyes. "Did I say something to your mom or your daughter that you're mad at me about?"

His face jerked back, like she had struck him. "What? No," he said, but didn't elaborate.

"Then what is it? The first time you saw me you practically eviscerated me with your eyes. Then you show up here, and I've gotta say, you're pretty friggin' rude for someone who wants to come into my house and get paid for doing work here." She folded her arms across her chest. "So, what is it? What did I do? Because if I did something wrong, I'd like the chance to apologize. If I didn't, and you're just always such a ray of sunshine, then I'll say goodbye again and ask you to leave my property because I'm hungry and my dinner's getting cold."

His nostrils flared as he ran his hand over the back of his neck, dropping his eyes from her glare. His long hair swished a little as he worked the crick out of his neck and his jaw did that tweaking thing again. Sage's eyes were drawn to the tattoo she saw winding its way up his forearm into the pushed-up sleeve of his shirt. She suddenly wanted to touch it.

When the hell did he become sexy? She chided herself for entertaining thoughts of how good-looking Rowan was and reminded herself that he was, in fact, a great big jerk. That fluttery feeling in her stomach was nothing more than a lack of food. Which was also messing with her head.

She really needed to eat something.

Fast.

Rowan

Weeks of hating this woman had brought him to that moment. She called him on his bullshit. Of course she was angry with him. Why wouldn't she be? He'd spent every second of every day hating her since he learned she existed. Seeing her, being that close to her, was supposed to make it easier to think of her as his enemy, not harder.

Every word she said held up a big fucking mirror on the childish behavior he'd been throwing at her. He might as well have reached out and pulled her braids. Rowan had to choose, keep acting like a pouting toddler, or act like the professional he was and help the woman with the work she needed to have done. It was not his house. It never was his house.

"You didn't do anything wrong," he said, his voice coming out harder than he meant it to. "I've just had a pretty rough couple of weeks. There was no need to take any of it out on you, though." He shoved his hands into his back pockets to give them something to do as he held her angry gaze. "I'm really sorry, Miss Lowery." Her eyes grew wide at the use of her last name. "I was serious when I said you need to have the electrical work taken care of, and any plumbing you need as well, before you have anything else done. I won't blame you one bit if you want to hire a different electrician, but that stuff has to be taken care of."

"You can just call me Sage." Her tone wasn't friendly but wasn't as hostile as it had been a minute ago.

He nodded his understanding, grabbed his phone and scrolled through to grab Joe Kemp's number for her. When he looked back up, she was watching him with a curious look in her eye. It was as if she had him under a microscope and he was stuck where he was until she had seen enough to make up her mind about him.

"You know a lot about this house?" she asked.

"Nick and I were friendly," Rowan said. "My daughter used to like to come down here and keep the old guy company while I worked around the house and fixed little things for him. He was pushing eighty and I liked helping him out. And when you hang around a place often enough you pick up on the things that need to be fixed."

It wasn't an outright lie, more of a re-shaping of the truth. A lie of omission, not commission. The things he told her were true. He simply chose to leave out the part about wanting to fix the place up for himself and Maisie—not her.

One side of her face lifted in a half smile as she uncrossed her arms and slid her hands into the pockets of her hoodie.

"What?" he asked. "What kind of face is that?" *A beautiful one*, his brain answered out of nowhere. *With really soft-looking lips. Kissable lips*, it added unhelpfully.

"It's nothing," she said. "I'm just having a hard time imagining you being nice to someone." She tilted her head, regarding him with that microscope gaze again. "Or was that your daughter's job? She's the sweetness to counteract your sour?" Her eyebrow lifted, challenging him to defend himself. Except he had no defense.

"Something like that," he said. "You're a hundred percent right about my daughter, though. She absolutely is the sweetest person I know." Not wanting to get too personal, he switched back to the task at hand. He scrolled through his phone and said, "Here, let me send you the contact info for the other electrician." He texted Joe's information to her, and the text notification chimed from her back pocket.

Without taking her eyes from him she leaned back against the door, rested one foot on the edge of the threshold, her posture already more relaxed. "Thank you," she said. "But, before I call this other person, do you have time for this job? Meaning, if I choose to hire you, will you actually show up here to get this work done, or am I going to have to wait weeks in between each project?"

He thought about the job at the Faraway Inn where he and Marcus would be most days for the next couple months. One of the local inns had recently changed ownership and was in the process of a major remodel, including building out a bar and a restaurant. It was a big job, but something about having another electrician doing the work in this house didn't sit well with him. Mostly he didn't want someone else in what should have been his house. And in a part of his brain he didn't want to acknowledge, he didn't want someone else in the house with Sage.

"As it happens, my schedule is pretty full over the next couple months, but if you don't mind me coming over in the evenings, kind of like tonight, I can certainly get this done for you."

"How long do you think it will take to get it all done after hours?"

Rowan lifted his chin, indicating the door against which she leaned. "Well, I need to get inside first and make an accurate list of what needs to be done so I can make a materials list and a time estimate. Then I'll put it all together for you and send over a formal estimate."

Looking at him for an extra heartbeat, which had him ready to say, *Forget it. Call Joe,* she finally pushed herself away from the door and said, "OK. Let's do this." She opened the door and entered in front of him. A soft lavender scent wafted into his nostrils as he followed behind her and his eyes dropped to check out her ass. Unfortunately, there wasn't much to look at since whatever she had back there was hidden beneath a giant hoodie.

Rowan

Walking inside the house now that Nick was gone was a surreal experience. When the old man lived there, Rowan would imagine his own sofa in place of the old blue striped one that sat in the living room, and a kitchen full of new stainless-steel appliances instead of the black and chrome stove and the plain white refrigerator. Because it was only Nick living there, he had never installed a dishwasher. That was on the top of the priorities list for Rowan. At least it had been before Sage Lowery showed up.

Sage walked through the empty living room and sat at a small table in the kitchen, grabbing a slice of pizza from the counter as she did. It was the kind of small, plastic table his parents used to set up when their friends would come over to play cards. The two chairs looked like they were taken from a patio set, with their green mesh fabric and hollow metal arms.

It was a strange dichotomy to see a woman so sure of herself sitting at a makeshift patio set in her kitchen.

"You don't mind if I eat some of my dinner, do you?" she asked. He half expected her to offer him a piece of the pizza. She didn't.

"No, of course not," he said. "Do you mind if I just take some notes on what needs to be done in each room?"

"As long as I can sit here and eat while you do it." She leaned back in one of the lawn chairs and stretched her feet out in front of her, crossing her legs at the ankle. For the first time, Rowan noticed the Nordic style of her socks. With her long, almost black hair, he never would have picked her for being Nordic in any way. It was an interesting look for her.

"Be my guest," he said. "I'll start upstairs if that's OK with you."

She nodded. He still couldn't figure out what was so intriguing about this woman. From her super casual clothes and her intense bearing and defensive nature to her random-ass patio set in her kitchen but no furniture to be seen anywhere else, he just didn't know what to think.

As he walked through the hallway to the stairs, he felt her eyes on him, but when he turned around to look, she was scrolling through her phone with one hand and holding a half-eaten slice of pizza with the other.

Seeing all the work she'd already done upstairs smashed his heart all over again. It was supposed to be him doing the work up there. It was supposed to be him ripping out the nasty rugs and peeling off the ugly wallpaper. He was supposed to be doing that for Maisie. The room that Nick always used as a closet was supposed to be his office and the room at the back of the house was supposed to be hers.

Gripping his pencil so tightly it almost snapped, he quickly noted the few things that needed to be done up there, then returned to the safer space of the first floor. He started taking notes in the living room.

"Do you have plans to put any window unit air conditioners in this room?" he asked.

"I was thinking of putting one in that window there." She pointed to the same window where he had planned on putting one.

"Good choice. I'd have done the same."

She quirked an eyebrow at him. "Cool," she said then went to the fridge to grab a bottle of seltzer water. "Can I get you something to drink?" she asked. "I don't have much. Just some seltzer and a couple of ginger ales my friend left behind."

Rowan's brain seized on the word 'friend,' and he couldn't help but wonder if the friend was a female or a male. It was none of his business, but it didn't stop him from thinking about it. "No thanks," he said. "I just need to make a few notes in here and then I'll get the kitchen."

He had no idea how hard it would be to do this walk-through for someone else. Every place he looked was another smack in the face. Walking into the kitchen, he leaned his hip against the counter. "What are you thinking of doing in here?"

From her seat at the table, she craned her neck in a circle one way then back around the other way. "Aside from replacing all the appliances, the countertops, and the floor, I think this room just needs some new, updated outlets. Oh, no, wait. I think you said I needed a dedicated line for the microwave, right?"

"I think that's probably a good idea. How about a dishwasher? Are you thinking of putting one in?"

"I actually hadn't thought about it. It's only me and I don't make a ton of dishes. Do you think I should?"

The thought of living without a dishwasher was akin to torture as far as Rowan was concerned, but he couldn't very well say that to a client, especially one that barely tolerated his existence as it was. "I don't know, that's a call you have to make. But there's plenty of room for one if you want to put one in."

He walked over to the long counter that ran along the back wall next to the sink. "You'd have to take out this section of cabinet," he said pointing to the cabinet nearest the sink. "But then the dishwasher would just slide right in."

If he was a better man, his mind wouldn't have hung up on the thought of sliding things in. But he wasn't a better man, he was a man that was in a room with a beautiful woman, and it had been a hell of a long time since he'd slid anything anywhere.

He ignored his racing thoughts and cleared his throat. "But if you want to do it... install a dishwasher, that is... you'll need to let me know so I can run the line."

Looking at her, he couldn't tell if she was smiling in a nice way or planning to kill him in the kitchen and bury him in the backyard, but there was definitely something happening in her brain.

"I might as well put one in while everything is being done, right?" she said.

"Got it," he said, making a note of her decision. "The dining room and the laundry room don't need any electrical work, right? Just the replacement of the outlets?"

"Far as I know," she said. "Oh, I also want to have ceiling fans installed in my bedroom and the two rooms upstairs. Plus, I need to have a dedicated line for the A/C unit I want to put in my bedroom, right?" She half smiled at him. "Sorry. I just decided on the ceiling fans. I probably should have made that decision earlier."

He leaned against the counter again, writing down the additions to the job. "So, do you have a budget in mind for all this work?" he asked.

She took another slice of pizza from the counter, still without offering him one. "Not really. I thought you were going to give me a quote and then you'd do the work and I'd pay you. Isn't that how this kind of thing usually works?" She bit off a large piece of pizza and covered her mouth with her free hand while she chewed.

"I just meant, do you want to break up the job into sections, so you're not hit with a big bill all at once?"

Washing down her bite of pizza with a swig of seltzer, she said, "Oh. That." She shook her head. "No, just do whatever you do and bill me whenever you want. The sooner you're done, the sooner I can move on with the rest of the renovations."

"All right," he said, mentally noting with a tinge of resentment the carefree way she spoke about money. For someone who made a decent living and still struggled to buy a house for himself, her nonchalance hit him right in the ego. "Let me take a look in the bedroom and bathroom," he said. "Then I'll be out of your hair for the night."

When Nick was living there, Rowan had only gone through the master bedroom once to get to the bathroom to fix the trap under the sink. He looked around the bedroom, noted the lack of curtains over the windows, the faded outlines where Nick's furniture had cast shadows on the walls, protecting sections from the bright sun. As with the rest of the house, Sage had no furniture in the bedroom, except for a blowup mattress against one wall. Several suitcases sat against the closet door, all closed and zipped shut.

Entering the bathroom, disappointment rolled over him again as all the *would've* and *could've* thoughts raced around his mind. He would've ripped out the stand-up shower stall and installed one of the whirlpool tubs, exactly the way Marcus suggested. He would've pulled out the ugly, and far too small, vanity and installed a double-sink vanity in its place with a large mirror above it. With Marcus's help, he could've installed it all and had the bathroom upgraded in a week.

The bathroom still held some of the scented steam from Sage's recent shower. He breathed it in and wondered if her skin would smell just as good, which led naturally to wondering if it would taste as good too. His dick reacted to his traitorous thoughts and his pants were suddenly too tight.

For a woman who showed up with three suitcases of belongings and no furniture to speak of, she certainly traveled with a shitload of toiletries. The vanity had been entirely covered with stuff. Bottles of shampoos and lotions and make up. Brushes and hair elastics. Toothpaste and a toothbrush next to a small plastic cup. A hair dryer sat on the floor next to it. Maisie would have a field day hanging around with Sage Lowery and all her girly crap. The thought brought an unexpected smile to his lips.

Fuck. He needed to get his head on straight. This was supposed to be his house. This was supposed to be his bathroom. And those were supposed to be Maisie's things all over the vanity. He needed to stop thinking about Sage Lowery outside of being a client. That's all she was. No matter how amazing her skin might smell... or feel... or taste, she was nothing to him outside of that.

"Is everything OK in here?" From behind him, Sage's voice made him jump. "Wow, sorry. Didn't mean to scare you." She leaned against the doorframe, arms folded across her chest, a borderline frown on her face. "Deep in thought about how much work the place needs?"

"No," he said. "I was just thinking how out of place all of this female stuff" he whirled his hands in the general direction of her toiletries, "looks in such an outdated, masculine-looking space. It made me laugh, thinking of what Nick would say about it all." Again, not a total lie, but not the entire truth either.

The bathroom was cramped with the two of them in there together. He needed space. Away from her. Away from this house. Space to screw his head back on right.

"I think I have everything I need," he said, stepping around her to go back down the hall toward the kitchen. "I'll work up the estimate and get it back to you in a few days."

Sage

She'd had a few days to make some more progress before Rowan emailed over his estimate. Scanning it quickly, she didn't see anything that stood out as unreasonable.

> This looks fine

> How soon can you start?

The following Friday evening, Rowan showed up a few minutes before his scheduled six-thirty start time. She had already cleaned up the tools she'd used to patch the holes in the plaster walls in the second-floor guest room, taken her shower, and eaten a quick dinner of microwave lasagna for one.

When he knocked on the door, she was prepared to ignore how attractive he was. What she wasn't prepared for was how good he smelled as he walked past her into the house. His hair was slightly damp and the scent of whatever soap he'd washed himself in tickled something in her brain, which was directly connected to her center, and she was slightly shocked at her body's reaction.

"I'm going to start in the master bathroom, if that's alright with you," he said, carrying in his toolbox, leaving her following in his wake of spicy pine forest.

"Sure," she said. "I'll be in the kitchen if you need anything." She spent her time editing photos and scheduling social media posts. Most importantly, she'd kept herself busy, and kept her thoughts, and her body, a reasonable distance from Rowan.

Lost in her edits and lighting fixes, she didn't hear him until he spoke. "If you don't mind me asking, where'd you move from?"

"Boston," she said, looking up from her laptop to see him leaning his solid body against the kitchen doorway. "Technically, Brookline. But close enough." He didn't need to know more about her, so she left it at that.

He wasn't done. "What made you move all the way out here? Did you get a new job or something?"

How did she answer that? *I have terrible judgment when it comes to guys, so I ran away on a whim to the Berkshires to get away from them?* "I'm a photographer," she said finally, deciding on a partial truth. "I work wherever I find myself." She was going to end it there, but found herself adding on, "I needed a break from the city. A little time to decompress."

"Decompress from what?" he said, walking further into the kitchen, closer to her.

The way he looked at her unnerved her. He wasn't scary, but his expressions bordered on severe. Or maybe a better word would be intense. It wasn't easy to categorize him, but one thing was certain, spending too much time looking into eyes like that could get a girl burned.

Been there, done that. Thanks, but no thanks.

"Stuff," she said.

"Stuff," he repeated. "Gotcha." He leaned against the counter, completely comfortable and at home. She imagined he had probably stood in that exact spot with that exact posture countless times when his friend owned the house. But it wasn't his friend's house anymore. It was her house.

Completely against the personal need to keep Rowan Kennedy at a distance, the professional in her wanted to capture the moment of him standing there, out of place but entirely comfortable to be so, and she scanned the counter for her camera.

As if reading her thoughts, he said. "So, you're a photographer? What kind of photography do you do? Weddings and stuff like that?"

"I used to do weddings, but they were way too high stress for me," she confided. "They paid well, but I never had the patience for the ridiculously stressed-out brides. I do more commercial work now. Head shots, corporate and commercial advertising, and stuff like that. I do real estate on occasion, which I like. My best friend is an agent and I work with her every now and again."

"That's cool," he said.

Talking about her job made it more real in the moment again. "Yeah," she said. "It's pretty fun. Speaking of photography and what I do, I was wondering if you'd mind if I took some shots of you while you work around the house?"

His eyes narrowed and he regarded her with that deep, intense gaze. "Why?" His reaction told her that wasn't a request he'd probably ever gotten before.

"It wouldn't be just you," she threw out. "Like I said, I'm a photographer, and I'm documenting the renovations on the house. I edit the best ones and share them out on my socials. It's a way to keep my name out there, make sure companies remember I exist while I'm out here."

His hair had fallen into his face, and he flipped it back with the jerk of his head. "Maybe," he said. "I'll let you know."

It was a sudden power shift in their dynamic. She had been the one in charge. It flip-flopped with a single word: *Maybe.* He had something she wanted, and he knew it. She had a feeling he wasn't going to make it easy on her.

If that was his game, she would tell him to forget it. She'd get pictures of the plumber, and hope he was even half as good looking as Rowan was.

"Speaking of the renovations," he said. "Can I ask who you've got coming in to do the work? I know pretty much all the construction crews in the area."

Sage squared her shoulders and pulled herself up to her full five-foot-seven height, which was well short of his six-foot-whatever stature, but she did it anyway. "Actually," she said, "aside from things like the plumbing and electrical work that I can't do, I had planned on doing the rest of the work myself."

She wanted to smack that stupid smirk off his face. "Why is that funny to you?" she asked, irritation rising in her voice. "I told you, I'm a photographer. I'll be documenting everything I do as I go."

"Right," he said. "You mentioned that part. But what about the things you don't know how to do?" He lifted his hand and started ticking things off on his fingers. "Things like installing new appliances, installing the closet systems, sanding down and refinishing the wood floors, knocking down the water damaged wall in the laundry room and rebuilding it... You know how to do any of that?" He took two steps closer to her.

"No," she admitted. "But that's what Google is for," she said, holding up her phone and waving it at him as she moved closer to him. "I'll figure stuff out as I need to know it."

Her brain battled between wanting to shove him out the front door and wanting to push him against the counter and kiss that irritating look right off his face, in equal measure. *He is not the guy for you,* her brain reminded her. *You're not here for that. You're here to get away from that. It doesn't matter that he makes your whole body burn just by being near him. You are shit at choosing guys. Shove him out the front door. Now. Before you say or do something stupid.*

Taking another step toward her, he pulled her in and crushed his mouth over hers. There was no tenderness, only heat, and Sage welcomed it, felt her body ignite and waited to be consumed by it.

Rowan's tongue pushed into her mouth, sweeping through, tangling with hers as his hands gripped her hair and tilted her head back, allowing him access to her mouth, her jaw, her neck, which he devoured with equal ferocity.

Sage's arms crossed behind his neck, pulling their bodies together, feeling the heat swirling around them before she remembered that she didn't like this man. Why, then, was it so easy to kiss him and let his hands roam her body, down her back, over her ass? Why didn't she push him out the front door when she had the chance?

Before she could say anything, he stoked the fire in her belly by rubbing circles against her responding nipples and she let her head fall back with a gasp.

Needing to feel the heat of his skin, she reached around and slipped her hands under his shirt, kneading her fingers into the taut muscles of his lower back.

The sore muscles from hours of work, the unending to-do list on her phone, the uncertainty of the past few months as well as the future before her all melted away under the heat of Rowan Kennedy's kiss. Her breasts ached for his touch as he continued to stroke and tease her through her shirt. She pressed against him, and he responded with a grunt, spun them around and pushed her against the wall, his arousal hard against her belly.

She barely had time to think about what to do next. Was she supposed to ask about a condom? Was that his job? Did she even have condoms? The ringing of the phone in his back pocket brought all her thoughts to a screeching halt as she put her hands against his chest, pressed his body away from hers a fraction. "You should probably answer that."

Rowan lowered his mouth to kiss her jaw, up to the shell of her ear. "They'll call back," he said, and she turned to meet his mouth with her own, needing to taste him, to have his tongue in her mouth again. She hoped to God one of them had a condom and she could get more of him inside her, when the phone rang again.

With a frustrated sigh, Rowan pulled away, but still kept her pinned in place by the weight of his hips against hers and yanked the phone from his back pocket. "Fuck," he said, stepping away from her, running a hand through his messy hair. "It's Maisie," he said but didn't swipe to answer the phone. "I need a minute before I can talk to her."

She didn't know if she should be relieved that they would have to stop or pissed off that they couldn't finish what they'd started. The pounding need between her legs screamed for release while her rational brain reminded her that Rowan was not the man for her despite that sexy as sin body and the way he kissed her like he could kiss her forever.

"Hey, baby girl," Rowan said into his phone, swiping a hand over the scruff on his face; the same scruff that Sage wanted to feel against every inch of her skin. "What's up?"

Sage couldn't hear all of the conversation, only the high pitch of Maisie's little girl voice as she told Rowan whatever it was she needed to say. She walked out of the room to give her brain time to clear.

"All right, I'll be home in a few minutes. Tell Gramma I said you can wait up until I get there, and I'll read you a story before bed," Rowan said as he followed Sage into the living room. He paused, listening. "No, Zee, not three stories. One story."

Sage smiled as he tried to sound like he was the one in charge, knowing full well he'd end up reading her three stories.

"I'll see you in a little bit… I love you, too." He clicked to end the call and shoved the phone into his pocket. "I'm really sorry about that," he said.

Sage brushed her hair back over her shoulders, tried to act like it was no big deal. She crossed her arms as he approached. "Don't even worry about it," she said, trying to brush it off like it was the most natural thing in the world to be so close to having sex with someone and then having a metaphorical bucket of ice water dumped over your head. "It's probably better that we stopped anyway." She fidgeted, shifting her weight from one foot to the other as he closed the distance between them.

His expression was hard, his mouth set in an unsmiling line across his face. After a quick nod, he said, "Will you be around tomorrow, late afternoon? I can come by and get started on the line for the air conditioner in your bedroom."

"Yeah," she finally answered, her brain deep in thought about the two of them heating up her bedroom enough to need an air conditioner. "I'll be here all day. I was planning to work in the guest bath tomorrow, see about getting the old tile up so I can get a plumber in to install a shower. And maybe rip down the mirror and the cabinets and stuff." She rambled as her nerves wrought havoc with her ability to communicate a simple yes or no answer.

It was definitely for the best that he had to leave, otherwise she would have let the situation play out to its natural conclusion and now that she had a minute to think on it, perhaps it wasn't the best decision she could have made. Watching Rowan walk out the door was the hardest, but ultimately best, thing that could have happened.

Sage

For the entire next week, Sage managed to find things to do to make sure she was out of the house when Rowan came by to work. A drawn-out trip to the grocery store, a sudden interest in exploring the downtown area, including several trips to her new favorite art consignment store, Happenstance, as well as a newfound interest in gardening all kept her busy and out of his line of sight.

Julia surprised her with a quick visit, showing up right before dinner on Friday night. "I have the whole weekend to hang out!" she said as they sat together, a pitcher of sangria between them, at the small metal bistro table and chairs Sage had picked up during the week.

"I've been wanting a set out here since you showed me the photos that night at dinner. What do you think?" she asked Julia. "It fits, right?"

"Perfect," Julia said, raising her sangria glass in the air for a one-sided toast. "I can't believe how much you've gotten done in a couple of weeks. Those rooms upstairs are almost unrecognizable. The next time I come back, I won't even remember what they used to look like."

The women had put the leftover pizza in the refrigerator and decided to enjoy the early summer evening on the front porch. When she was alone, Sage only drank seltzer, but having Julia there felt like a celebration, and the sangria went down like juice.

"Hi, Miss Sage," a little voice called from somewhere off to their right. The distinct sound of plastic training wheels spinning and bouncing off the sidewalk as they approached at high speed made Sage smile. Leaning forward to look down toward Maisie, she expected to see Delores walking behind her, and saw the broad, looming body of Rowan instead.

"Hi, Maisie," Sage said as Maisie came to a halt in front of the fence. "Looks like you won't be needing those training wheels for much longer."

A second later, Julia gasped as Rowan appeared next to Maisie. "Oh," she whispered from behind her glass. "Who is that beautiful man? Please tell me you know him."

"Hey, Sage," he said.

"Rowan." Her belly flip-flopped and beside her, Julia cleared her throat. "Rowan, this is my friend, Julia. Julia, this is my neighbor, Rowan, and his daughter, Maisie. He and Maisie live over there," she said pointing up the road to the big white house.

"Nice to meet you, Rowan," Julia said with way too sultry a voice. "Nice to meet you, too, Maisie," she added in her regular Julia voice.

"Rowan is also the electrician doing all the work in the house," Sage said, trying to keep her tone casual.

"Oh, that's great," Julia said. Then she added under her breath, "Lucky you."

Sage had to hold back her laugh as Rowan became noticeably un-comfortable with Julia's pretend flirting. He coughed unnecessarily. "Work's coming along pretty well in there, I noticed," he said, lifting his chin toward the house. "I haven't seen you much to tell you, but it looks good."

Beside her sangria glass, Julia snickered and whispered, "*He* looks good."

Trying her best to ignore Julia, Sage nodded at Rowan. "Thanks," she said. "You coming back again Monday?"

"Yeah. I'll be back same time as normal."

The tension in the air between the three adults was comical. Julia was freaking Rowan out and trying her hardest to embarrass Sage. Sage was doing her best not to notice the way his dark gray t-shirt clung to his biceps or the way his hair brushed the collar of his shirt while, at the same time, ignoring Julia's open flirting. And Julia seemed to be having the time of her life causing mischief and discomfort all around.

"Ready to go, Zee?" Rowan asked, giving his daughter's back a gentle nudge.

"Bye, Miss Sage," she called out as she pushed her legs, one by one, down on the pedals, the bike wobbling with her efforts. "My grandma wants you to come to our house," she yelled out as she finally found her balance again and pedaled away from the driveway.

Julia cracked up and fell back into her chair, throwing her feet up onto the railing before she refilled her sangria, and said, "How have you not moved on that man yet? Good Lord, did you see his arms? Those arms could hold a girl steady while he did a lot of nice things to her..." With her free hand, she fanned herself, lying back dramatically in the chair.

"Haven't noticed," Sage said, returning to her own seat.

"You are such a terrible liar," Julia said as she poured the rest of the pitcher into Sage's cup. "You would literally have to be blind to not notice him. And the fact that he's in your house every night and you haven't made a move? I think I might need to check your pulse to make sure you're still alive."

Sage swallowed a mouthful of sangria. "I told you, Jules, I'm here to fix up my house, not hit on the guy doing the electrical work."

"But you have seen him, right?"

Sage laughed. "Yes, of course I've seen him." Her face pulled into a frown. "A girl would have to be dead not to have seen him."

"I knew it! I knew you liked him."

"Like him? Who said I like him?" Sage asked, turning to stare with wide eyes. "I said he looks good. That doesn't mean I like him. He's actually kind of a jerk."

Giggling, no doubt from three glasses of sangria, Julia said, "Oh yes, I could tell from the gentle way he was teaching his small daughter to ride her bicycle that he is just one terrible monster. Now I see why you don't like him."

Reaching over, Sage playfully hit Julia in the arm. "I didn't say he was always a jerk. He's just always a jerk to me. And I've had more than enough of that. So, yes, I will watch him work, and I will enjoy seeing his ass in those jeans and his arms in those t-shirts, but no, I will not make a move on him, ask him on a date, or do any other thing which would give him the impression that I am in any way interested in him."

And she certainly wouldn't let anything like that volcanic kiss in the kitchen happen again.

The longer she spoke, the more confident she felt, almost to the point of believing her own words. "I am focusing my efforts right now on things that don't have a penis!"

Julia snort-laughed and had to put her glass down on the porch so she didn't spill it. When she eventually stopped laughing, she said, "I think you might be making a mistake there, because I'd put money on that penis being pretty frickin' epic!"

Rowan

"Daddy," Maisie said, letting her feet rest on the pedals as Rowan guided her up the driveway. "I thought you said you like Miss Sage."

He stood tall, stretching the ache out of his low back. "What do you mean? I already told you I like her just fine."

From under her helmet, she stared at him. "Then how come you're not very nice to her?"

Her words bothered him. Not that she'd said them, but that his behavior toward their neighbor brought them out of her. He hadn't thought he'd been rude. Quiet and uncomfortable as hell, but not rude.

His job as Maisie's dad meant raising her to be a better person than he was, so at least he was getting that part right. But it also meant setting a better example for her than he'd been doing. Seeing himself through the eyes of a watching five-year-old offered him a perspective with which he wasn't entirely comfortable.

All of a sudden, his decision to kiss Sage the week before seemed like a dick move. He'd been nothing but an asshole, then he kissed her with no warning, just following his gut instinct. No wonder she'd been busy doing other things every time he'd been there since.

Once they walked into the house, Rowan helped Maisie take off her socks and shoes, though she didn't need his help anymore. Crouching before her with one shoe in his hand, he said, "You're right about Miss Sage. Daddy could be a whole lot nicer to her. I'm sorry."

"That's OK, you can try again tomorrow." She got up from the bench, hurried toward the living room, and plopped herself in her beanbag chair. "Can I watch Curious George until dinner's ready?"

"Sure, baby girl."

"What was that all about?" his mother asked as he entered the kitchen to wash his hands so he could help chop vegetables. His sister and nephew would be coming over for dinner, so he grabbed a few extra veggies from the fridge.

"Nothing."

"Were you not nice to a client? That's not like you." She sprinkled salt, pepper, and garlic powder over the chicken in the baking dish. "Did something happen?"

She never changed her expression so Rowan didn't know if he should be on the defensive or just answer her question. Tossing the cucumbers into the salad bowl, he said, "No, nothing happened. It's all my own shit. I'm just having a tough time working in that house, is all. Every-fucking-where I look, I see what I wanted it to be and now I have to make it something else for someone else." He was careful to keep his voice low because Maisie had no idea about his plans for that house.

"What did you want Mr. Nick's house to be?" Maisie yelled from the living room.

He obviously didn't keep it low enough.

His mother gave him a sympathetic smile. "Maisie, honey, why don't you go upstairs and wash up before Auntie and Finn get here, OK?" she said. "Daddy and Grandma are talking about grownup stuff."

"I like grownup stuff," she said, in a matter-of-fact tone.

"Maisie," Rowan warned.

"Fine," she said. "But can I wait until this show is over?"

Rowan and Delores finished getting dinner ready while Maisie's show played out. After giving up on hearing anymore grownup talk, she went upstairs to wash.

"So," Delores said, once Maisie was out of earshot. "What happened with you and Sage?"

"Honestly, nothing. Well, not entirely nothing. We kissed the other night but that was a big fucking mistake and we've pretty much been ignoring it like it never happened. Then there's this low-level irritation every time I'm over there," he said. "I see the things I wanted to do in the house and she's doing all different things and it's kind of killing me." He hadn't stopped thinking about their kiss and that pissed him off too.

There was also the whole money issue, but he probably sounded petty enough in his mother's ears without adding that to the mix.

Delores opened her mouth to speak but Rowan cut her off.

"I know that's stupid," he said. "I know it's her fucking house." He dropped the knife to the counter and slid the peppers into the bowl on top of the cucumbers. "I understand it makes no logical sense, but that's how it is." He stacked a few stalks of celery and started to slice them.

"She seems like a very nice woman," Delores said, entirely missing the point of Rowan's resentment.

"She's pretty too," Maisie said, appearing like a ninja behind them.

Rowan jumped, the knife clattering onto the counter. "Jesus Christ, Maisie!"

"That's another dollar," she yelled, running toward the rapidly filling swear jar.

Sage

She loved having company, but found she looked forward to the work ahead of her now that Julia had gone back to Boston. The progress she was making was edging toward two finished rooms upstairs, instead of being two stripped down empty spaces. Rather than have the floors refinished, she covered them with large area rugs and let the rustic look of the floors beneath show around the edges.

All she needed to do was paint and decorate and she could move her bedroom temporarily to the guest room then get to work on the first floor.

Normally by the time Rowan showed up to work, Sage was cleaned up and doing other things so as not to be in the same space. But she was so close to having the guest room finished, she thought it worth the risk of spending time around him. Besides, she was a grown woman, more than capable of keeping her hands to herself.

She bit her lip to keep from laughing out loud when he walked into the house, and Julia's admiration of him and his potentially epic penis, popped into her brain. What she never told Julia was that she knew what he was hiding in those pants because it had been solid and pressed against her the night they kissed.

"You sticking around tonight?" he asked, lifting his toolbox to the kitchen counter. "That's not like you."

Was he teasing her? Or was he flirting with her?

"Nowhere to go," she said, unsure what to say next. Should she flirt back or just be casual? But how did she stay casual when he was staring at her like he was waiting for her to say something. And the little smile that played at the corners of his mouth? What the hell was that all about? "I have some painting to do and some shelves to install in the office room closet tonight so I'll be out of your way in a second," she finally said.

"That's cool," he said. "If you need any help, just give me a yell. I'll be working in the kitchen tonight, running a new line for the microwave."

Who was this strange new person who'd taken over Rowan's body? And why did he throw Sage off her game? She was supposed to let him in, then go about her business. He was supposed to ignore her and go about his own. He wasn't supposed to be flirty, as much as it seemed possible for him anyway. And he really needed to stop looking at her that way, it was making her warm all over.

"Great," she said, heading toward the stairs with a glass of lemonade. "Thanks."

Thanks? That was the best she could come up with? She shook her head as she walked up the stairs.

Once she got to work, ignoring him was easy. In the span of an hour, she was able to put a finish coat of paint on the baseboard and around the door. Sitting back on her heels she looked over the work she'd done and nodded appreciatively. Each step brought her closer to her goal.

The next thing to do was install the white wire shelving in the closet, put up the curtain where the bi-fold doors used to be, and the room would be ready for a rug and some furniture. She'd already ordered a new desk and chair which was supposed to be delivered in the next few days. The finished room was starting to take shape in her mind, and she was excited to see it in real life.

As her excitement grew, she needed a change in her background music. The calm music she needed to keep a steady hand as she painted wasn't needed anymore. A little Dropkick Murphys would be the perfect soundtrack for the last bit of work in the office.

Her phone was on the top of the ladder in the middle of the room, so she hopped back up to her feet. Or at least she tried to. Without realizing her foot had fallen asleep, Sage took a step toward the ladder and tripped when her sleeping foot refused to hold her up.

The next five seconds were the slowest of her entire life. Knowing she was falling toward the ladder but not able to stop herself, she tried to twist her body away from it but ended up reaching toward it and pulling it down on top of herself. Then she smashed her back onto something solid and thumped to the ground in a painful heap. A burning sensation started across her low back, and she pushed herself upright just as Rowan's footsteps pounded up the stairs.

Shit. Her hip throbbed and her back burned, though from what she wasn't sure yet. Feeling like a total idiot, the last thing she wanted was for Rowan to come charging through the door and see her sprawled out in a heap of wire shelving and paint cloths.

"Sage," Rowan yelled as he reached the top of the stairs. "Are you all right?" His big body filled up the small room as he ran through the door, jumped over the can of paint she'd been using, and crouched down beside her, offering his hands to help her get back to her feet. "Are you hurt?" he said, his eyes scanning her body for injuries.

Sage attempted to lift the ladder back to standing but Rowan moved around her. "I'll get that," he said. "You just stay still a minute and get your bearings."

As embarrassed as she was, she appreciated his help, nonetheless. "Thanks," she said, aware of the familiar burning tingle of her foot waking up. "I didn't realize my foot had fallen asleep and when I tried to walk on it..." Twisting her arm behind her back, she felt the tear in the fabric of her shirt then hissed in a breath at the sting of her fingers against the abraded skin.

Rowan's worried look was sexy as hell, which only made her more frustrated with herself. She wasn't there to be taken care of, but his concern still made her feel good. *He'd help anyone who'd hurt themselves,* she scolded herself mentally. *It's nothing special about you.*

"Turn around," he said. "I need to see if we have to get you to the ER." His tone left no room for argument.

She didn't think it was bad enough to need intervention but being in a location she couldn't see, he would be able to tell right away if the cut needed professional medical care. Turning her back to him, she closed her eyes, wishing it to be no big deal.

His fingers pulled at the cut in the shirt then stilled. "I don't think it's all that bad, but it's a little scraped up back here." He was quiet for a few seconds. "Do you know what you hit it on? I'm guessing the edge of the paint can over there."

She nodded. "Yeah, pretty sure that's what it was."

"You're lucky you only scraped the edge and didn't land directly on it. You might have broken a rib. But we definitely need to get this cleaned up. Come on," he said, handing over her phone, which he'd picked up for her. "Let's get you downstairs." Lowering his hand to the top of her hip, he gently guided her out of the room. When they made it downstairs to the bathroom, she expected him to walk away and let her take care of her injury by herself. Instead, he followed her inside.

If she thought his body took up all the space in the office room, he filled every available crevice of the bathroom, including all the oxygen she needed to breathe. "You don't need to worry about me," she said. "I can handle it from here."

Catching her eye in the mirror, he said, "Oh, really? How's that going to work when you can't even see what you're dealing with?" At his stern look that made her belly all kinds of wobbly, she nodded and agreed to let him help. "Where are your first aid supplies?" he asked, reaching toward the shelves behind the big mirror.

"Not back there," she said. "Actually, I don't know that I have any first aid supplies."

His stern look quickly morphed into a full-on scowl. "With all the work you're doing here, all the tools and all the ways you could possibly get hurt, you don't have at least a basic first aid kit? I don't have to tell you what a stupid thing that is, do I? Because that's pretty foolish."

Chastened, she knew he was right, but it didn't mean she wanted to admit it. "Gee, thanks, Dad. I'll be sure to buy some antibiotic lotion when I go out tomorrow, OK?"

His eyebrows rose, challenging her with a look. "Are you getting sassy with me, young lady?"

She couldn't help but laugh. "No, sir."

"Good," he said. "Stay here a second. I've got a small kit in my toolbox. Enough to get this cleaned up anyway."

Rowan

When he came back with the first aid kit, Sage was twisting all around trying to see her back. She had lifted her shirt partway up her belly and the sight of her skin sent his thoughts racing. Wanting to reach out and touch what looked like petal soft skin, he gripped the kit tighter in his hand. "Alright," he said. "Turn around and keep your shirt off your back for a second."

His instructions didn't call for her to stand with her hands against the counter and her ass pushed slightly back, but since that's the way she heard them, he didn't argue. Instead, he enjoyed finally getting to see what she was always hiding under that baggy sweatshirt. And it was awesome. Full hips, and a nice ass that practically begged to be squeezed.

Reaching around her, he turned the sink on, waited for the water to warm up. Her body moved slightly toward his, her shoulder lightly resting against his chest. Her breath hitched when he accidentally grazed her breast as he scrunched a clean washcloth under the running water.

He was only supposed to be helping her clean up a cut, not getting turned on by the smell of her shampoo and the swell of her breast against his arm. His dick sure as hell was not supposed to be liking it as much as it was.

While she held her shirt slightly up, he carefully washed the scrape. She hissed a breath each time the cloth touched her. "You OK?"

"Fine," she said. "It just hurts a little."

"Almost done," he said, laying the cloth on the countertop and waiting for her skin to dry. "I'll put a little antibiotic lotion on it, but I think one Band-Aid should be enough." He caught her eye in the mirror and the way her lip was caught up between her teeth was the cutest shit he'd seen in a long time. He'd had hangnails worse than the scratch on her back but somehow, he wanted to make her feel better. He wanted her to remember the way he touched her and cared for her.

Shocked by his own thoughts, he snapped his focus back to her scrape, then covered it with a Band-Aid. "All done," he said. "See, it wasn't really a big deal."

What did feel like a big deal was the heat burning in her eyes as she turned from the sink and faced him head-on. Without thought he reached out to gently touch her face before he leaned down and placed his lips on hers.

"Oh," she whispered, but didn't pull away from him. He trailed a few soft kisses along her jaw then brought his mouth back to hers. She parted her lips for him, allowed his tongue to gently sweep into her mouth, tasting the sweetness of lemonade on her lips, cupping the sides of her face as his fingers twined into her long, silken ponytail.

He pulled back and watched her suck in her bottom lip as her eyes fluttered open. As reality dawned on her, she took a small step back from him and ran a finger along her puffy bottom lip. "Why did you do that?" she asked. "Why did you kiss me?"

He let out a slow breath to steady himself. "Honestly, I'm not sure," he said, then stepped closer because he suddenly had the need to stay near her. "It wasn't my intention when I offered to help." He ran a finger along her cheek, her eyes falling closed in response to his touch. "I haven't been able to stop thinking about your lips and what it was like kissing you last time."

"What was it like?" she asked, her eyes slowly opening and rising to meet his.

"Kissing you? Satisfying in every way." Leaning down he kissed her again. "Your lips are impossibly soft, and I enjoy kissing you more than I probably should."

"Why shouldn't you enjoy kissing me? Because I'm a client and you're doing work in my house, or is it some other ethical dilemma?" Her eyes flashed as she spoke, but her tone of voice told him she was teasing.

But she also wasn't wrong.

"Fuck," he said, taking a step back from her. "You're right, this is a mistake. You're a client and I never want you to feel uncomfortable having me here." It still killed him that this was her home, but he was slowly coming to terms with it. "I'm really sorry, Sage, I hope I didn't upset you." He hoped to hell he didn't just screw up in a major way.

This time it was Sage who closed the distance between them. "I'm totally kidding with you. I absolutely want you to finish the job—" Her words stopped mid-sentence as her eyes squeezed shut. Hiding her face behind her hands, she laughed. "That's so not what I meant," she said. "I mean I want you to finish the electrical work in my house. That's the job I want you to finish."

Swallowing down his own laugh, he said, "I don't get it. What else could you possibly want me to finish? Is there something else you'd like me to do?"

"Oh, my God," she said between laughs. "Stop teasing me. You know what I meant and now you're just trying to make me say something I'm not going to say."

He enjoyed watching her squirm.

But even as her words said she was embarrassed, her body told a different story. Her shoulders pushed back ever so slightly, and she pretended to swat at his chest but let her hand rest there until he took hold of it. Wrapping his fingers around her wrist, he pulled her closer with a tug she didn't resist.

Grabbing the back of his neck with her free hand, Sage hauled his face down, pressing her lips to his, initiating the hottest kiss he could bring to memory. Holding her wrist with one hand, he dropped the other to her ass, yanked her body closer to his as their tongues clashed. His heartbeat pounded in his ears and his balls tightened as he held onto her as tightly as a drowning man to a life raft.

He ached everywhere as he shifted his focus to her jaw and down the side of her neck, her sighs and gasps throwing fuel into the fire. Hands grasped and groped. She rubbed her body against his thigh, his hands firmly on her hips, enjoying the way they swayed with want and desire.

Sage

Like the first time they kissed, his rock-hard erection pressed against her body, but unlike the first time, Sage was confident she would know exactly how epic it was before he left.

With a growl, he reached down and ripped her shirt up over her head, tossing it to the floor, then dropped his mouth to her collar bone, grazed his teeth along her newly exposed skin.

One strong arm held her as she leaned back, giving him free reign to taste her, kiss her, lick her. He unhooked her bra, slid it off her shoulders and after tossing it to the pile with the shirt, began the blissful devouring of her breasts. She dug her fingers into his shoulders to keep her body upright while he licked and sucked her, teasing her with his tongue and fingers. The delicious tingle of desire and anticipation quickly engulfed her.

Dropping to his knees, he reached up and yanked her pants down her body, her panties coming off with them, leaving her naked against the sink and Rowan with his face directly in line with her center. The moan that escaped her when he pushed her legs apart and buried his face between her thighs wasn't her voice. It was a new voice, a different voice, the voice of some sex kitten that had taken over her body.

Keeping away from him had been so freaking difficult but giving in to her body's need for him was impossibly easy. She should have told him to stop but the word wouldn't form in her brain with his scruffy face scratching the soft skin of her inner thighs, his lips and tongue finding and enjoying her most intimate place.

He licked one deep stroke before he swirled his tongue around her clit, her legs quaking as they worked to keep her from collapsing to the ground. As he kissed and sucked her, he slid a finger deep inside and she accepted him with a rasping groan, rocking her hips against him, working against his face and his hand, the building energy rolling through her body, coiling in her midsection until she couldn't hold it back any longer.

The self-imposed denial she'd been living through was no match for the magic he worked on her willing body, crying out as her orgasm ripped through her like a shock wave.

He returned to his feet, his eyes locked onto hers as he pulled his shirt up and over his head, revealing the solid body beneath. Still shaky from her orgasm, Sage trailed her fingertips over his skin from his chest down to the button of his jeans. Rowan gently held her face as she slid her hands into his boxers and pushed everything down his hips, freeing his massive erection. Her breath caught as she admired the size of him, making a mental note that he was, in fact, epic.

Her body was loose and relaxed as she took hold of him with one hand, lowered to her knees, then took him as far into her mouth as she could. Rowan growled like an animal. She had never heard a man make a noise like that and it caused a whole new wave of heat to tear through her already charged up body. Working her tongue up the length of him, she licked small circles around the sensitive head while Rowan's hips started to sway with the smallest motion, pushing himself deeper into her mouth.

His fingertips cradled her head as she moved on him, taking him a little deeper each time, until, with no warning, he pulled out of her mouth with a grunt before kicking his shoes, jeans and boxers all the way off.

He was nothing short of magnificent and her appreciation of him didn't go unnoticed.

Like she weighed nothing, he scooped her into his arms and carried her into her bedroom. "That air mattress is toast if that's where we do this," he said, lowering her to the floor.

If she had been clear-headed, she would have been embarrassed about her furniture situation. But there was no time for that. She needed to have Rowan inside of her as soon as humanly possible. "We can just put the blanket on the floor," she said through ragged breaths.

Rowan whipped the blanket from the air mattress, laid it on the floor and knelt on it, pulling her down beside him, then very quickly rolling her beneath him. With his strong thighs he pressed her legs open wider and angled himself to enter her.

Before he did, Sage pulled her hips back slightly. "I'm on the pill," she said, stopping him momentarily. "And I'm totally clean. Please tell me you are too."

He locked gazes with her, his lips pulled into a smirk. "Well, I'm not on the pill, but I am clean."

"Oh, thank God." Her body relaxed, her legs falling open again, and welcomed him as he pressed against her opening and slowly slid himself in, stretching her. Her eyes rolled back as he pushed in all the way and the slight pain gave way to a greedy hunger for him to fuck her. Hard. Wrapping her legs around him, she used the leverage to grind her body against his while he pumped into her with increasing urgency.

Her fingers scratched his skin, caressed his back, his ribs, his neck—anywhere she could reach without opening her eyes, all the while feeling him move inside her. Turning her head to one side she kissed his arm, nipped at him, felt the warm skin and solid muscles of his forearms as they held his body above hers. The building spiral of orgasm started in her fingertips and toes, moving through her arms and legs until the friction of his pelvis grinding against hers set it free in a burst of overwhelming sensation.

She yelled his name as her body shook. He slammed into her again and again, a frantic pounding of body on body, flesh on flesh. A bead of sweat rolled down his cheek. His body stilled as he groaned. "Fuck!" he yelled, thrusting his hips as he came deep inside of her.

Rowan

Having fiercely hot sex with Sage was exactly what he needed. After more than two years of being alone, his body fell easily into the comfort of hers. It was also exactly what he shouldn't have wanted. Both thoughts fought for control of his mind, though he knew damn well which one controlled his dick.

He picked up the blanket and spread it out over her air mattress while he waited for her to come out of the bathroom. She emerged wearing a pair of baggy sweatpants and an oversize tee shirt, her feet still bare. Wisps of long dark hair hung free around her face, unable to stay in the messy knot on top of her head. The low light of her bedroom showed the light blush she still carried in her cheeks, and he wanted nothing more than to wrap his arms around her, pull her in for another round.

"I think we need to get you a real bed," he said.

"Yeah, it hasn't really been an issue until now. Sorry about that." Her fingers twisted into the hem of her shirt while she stared down at him. "I know you have to get back home, but I think we probably need to talk for a minute."

A loud thud sounded where his heart usually beat. Had he stupidly followed his dick and made the wrong choice? Again? "What's to talk about?" he said. "Aside from how perfectly we fit together."

She half smiled at his attempt to lighten the mood.

"We were pretty good together," she said, her fingers still wrapped in her shirt. "I don't know what it is about you that I just can't seem to resist. But I don't know if we should have done that." She took a half step toward him then stopped, her brows furrowing in thought. "Don't get me wrong, I've really wanted to do that since the day you kissed me," she said. "It's kind of all I thought about. But I have to be up front with you. I'm not looking for anything long term right now. I still haven't decided if I'm staying out here or selling the house and moving back to Boston." She blinked at him, her large eyes full of expectation, maybe even a hint of trepidation. "And I don't know how you feel about casual."

It wasn't the worst thing a woman had ever said to him, but he wasn't sure if it was a small thing either. He needed to be honest with her. "I don't know that I'm built for casual, Sage. Not when it feels like that just felt." He moved toward her slowly, reached out to pull her into his arms. "But if you want to try keeping things casual, we can do that," he said, resting his chin on top of her head.

"Really?"

"Really." It wouldn't be easy, she fit too perfectly against his body for that. He also knew what she tasted like and what she sounded like when he made her come, not easy things to put to the side for the sake of keeping things casual. "When I come here to work, that's it. I'll work and then go home. No expectations on either of our parts."

"OK." She nodded against his chest. "But what if you look really good and I want to have sex again?"

With a laugh, he said, "Not on work nights. If you would like to schedule time for that, let me know and I'll put you in my calendar."

She chuckled. "How romantic."

"Nope," he said, leaning back to look into her eyes. "The only way I'll be able to stick to our casual thing is by keeping romance out of it." He wanted to kiss the center of her forehead but that would already be breaking his brand-new no romance rule, so he held her gaze and waited instead.

Rolling her shoulders back and standing up straight, she said, "You're absolutely right. That is the only way to make this work." She withdrew her arms from around his waist and he silently cursed himself for agreeing to something so stupid as keeping things casual with her. It had only been ten minutes since he'd been inside her and he was ready to be with her again.

"I should get going. It's just about Maisie's bedtime," he said.

She walked him to the door but neither moved to hold the other's hand or display any sort of affection when they reached the door. It sucked and he hated it.

"I'll be back to do more work tomorrow," he said as his hand landed on the doorknob. His phone buzzed in his pocket.

> Ask Sage if she wants to come to dinner tomorrow

Not happening

> Ask her or I'll text her myself in three seconds

Rowan looked up at Sage, who simply stared at him, then returned to frantically typing. "Sorry," he said. "It's my mother."

> Don't do it she doesn't want to come to dinner

Then he heard it. The notification sound from the phone in Sage's pocket. She grabbed it, looked at it, quirked an eye in his direction. "It's also your mother," she said with a laugh. "Oh," she said then giggled. Why the hell would she be giggling?

"Sage, I'm sorry. My mother can be a bit overbearing. Just ignore her."

"I will not. That's rude." She typed something in reply and stuffed the phone back in her pocket.

She stood with her hand on the door frame. "Yeah, so, tomorrow night isn't going to work for me. Evidently your daughter has invited me to your house for dinner." She held up her phone and showed him the text, the faintest hint of a dimple in her right cheek as she tried not to smile.

"Just ignore them. She and my mother will have you over every week if they get their way. Really," he said, "I can tell them no if you're uncomfortable."

"Who said I was uncomfortable? Maybe I want to go to your house and eat dinner with your mother and your daughter. Is that weird or something?"

He couldn't win with any of the women in his life and it seemed Sage would be no exception.

Sage

The next morning, wrapped up in a comforter, Sage cradled her coffee, feet perched on the railing, and watched the sun climb higher into the sky. After Rowan had left, she jumped in to take a long, hot shower, then slept the sleep of the dead, not waking up until well past sunrise.

Her body enjoyed the awareness of everything that had happened the night before, calm, relaxed and a little bit sore, while her brain wrestled with her decision to have sex with him. For the time being she told her brain to be quiet and let her body enjoy its peaceful morning. They'd agreed to keep things casual, and she'd have to trust that they both meant what they'd said.

More of the flowers the previous owner had planted had started to come into bloom over the last week. As a homeowner, she should know what she was growing so she snapped a few photos with her phone and searched for the names of the plants. Within a few seconds, she learned she was the proud owner of a beautiful red columbine, several colors of hyacinth, as well as two lilac bushes that needed some love to help them bloom next year.

She pondered that for a second. That was the first time she imagined something about her new house further out than the end of the year. She hadn't thought about next year in any concrete terms before, but she liked it. She liked the idea of being in her house next year. She added 'learn about lilacs' to her list, then ran back into the house to grab her camera.

She spent an hour taking photos of the plants in her yard. Her plants. In her yard. She took them from as many angles and distance ranges as she could, including several from the ground looking up, with a rich, bright blue sky for a background.

Scanning through the digital display of photos while she stretched her legs on the front porch and sipped a glass of lemonade, Sage was filled with a sense of hope and contentment she hadn't felt since she left Boston. None of the pictures she had taken before that morning were even half as good as the ones she'd just captured. A thrill of purpose flooded her veins along with a thrill of anticipation at seeing Rowan again.

By the end of the day, the slanting rays of the afternoon sun told her it was time to get ready for dinner at Delores's house. Yes, it was Rowan's house too, but Delores and Maisie had invited her, not Rowan. Once she showered, she dressed in a pair of dark jeans and a loose coral-colored tank top, brushed a hint of blush onto her cheeks and dabbed on a speck of lip gloss. Her long hair would dry on its own, but she slipped a hair elastic into her pocket in case it decided to get frizzy as it dried.

The weather had taken a turn toward hot as June rolled into July, and the threat of an afternoon thunderstorm loomed in the darkening clouds to the north. Imagining herself sitting on her porch, bare feet propped on the white railing, watching the world turn gray as a thunderstorm rolled through held an almost primal appeal to her.

She grabbed her favorite zipper hoodie, along with her purse, as she headed out the door to eat dinner with her neighbors.

The early evening sun warmed her back, urging her toward the big white farmhouse that sat at the far end of a long driveway further back from the street than any of the other houses in the neighborhood. It was a beautiful, two-story home with a wraparound porch as well as a set of stairs leading to a side door. A two-car garage sat at the top of the driveway and looked like it might have been a later addition to the property as it didn't quite fit the age of the house itself.

She took a few deep breaths to get her heart rate back down as she neared the front porch, which was mostly blocked from view by large evergreen bushes. Approaching the front steps, she heard Rowan's voice in a strange falsetto. "Oh, no, Princess Maisie. Don't throw me in the dungeon for stealing your flying horse!"

Maisie's voice responded in a serious, deep tone, "I'm sorry villager. Stealing Pegasus is a crime and now I have no choice but to throw you in the dungeon."

As Rowan's villager voice called out, "Oh, no!" a Barbie doll came flying over the bushes, landing near Sage's feet and Maisie cackled like a girl mad with power.

Sage's laughter brought Rowan's and Maisie's faces over the top of the bushes as they peered down at her. Maisie jumped up and down. "Hi, Sage!" She turned to Rowan, who was brushing off his pant legs and pushing the toys into a pile with one foot. "Daddy, look! Sage is here to eat dinner with me!"

"I see that, baby girl." He smiled at Sage then crouched down to pick up the dolls from the pile and toss them into a plastic bin. "Come on, Zee, let's get this stuff picked up and back in your room, OK?"

He accepted the doomed villager from Sage's outstretched hand as she ascended the steps and handed it to him. "Here, don't forget this poor lady," he said to Maisie. "I think she needs a rest after her time in the dungeon."

Sage's gaze wandered over the scene as she took in the tenderness of the interaction between Rowan and Maisie. Her smile landed squarely on Rowan, and it pleased her to know he did, in fact, have a heart. A fairly soft one, it seemed.

"'K, Dad," Maisie said, taking the doll and dropping it unceremoniously into the plastic bin. "Can I show Miss Sage my room?"

"Not right now, she just got here. Maybe in a little while." He picked up the bin and placed it into Maisie's arms then opened the door for her. "All the way up to your room, please. I don't want them left on the stairs."

Maisie's back was to her, but Sage heard the sigh and could imagine the eye roll that went along with it as she stepped into the house. "Fine," she said and dragged her feet as she walked away.

"I do believe you have your work cut out for you in the years to come, Mr. Kennedy," Sage teased.

"I think you mean 'every single day,' Miss Lowery," he said, a cheeky grin firmly affixed to his face. Rowan hadn't shaved in a couple days and the stubble growing on his chin made funny things happen in Sage's belly, especially when he ran a hand through his hair, brushing the long strands out of his eyes. "Can I get you something to drink?" he asked. "I've got water. Wine. Beer?"

"Beer sounds great, thank you."

Rowan disappeared into the house while Sage took a seat on the top step and waited. He returned a minute later with two open summer ales in hand and sat down next to her while keeping noticeable distance between their bodies. They each sipped in silence. It was a nice silence, though. A companionable silence. A casual silence.

The pounding of Maisie's feet down the stairs, through the house, to the door brought matching smiles to their faces. "Gramma said to come inside," she said through the screen and then turned and ran away again.

Dinner was a perfect summer combination of burgers from the grill, homemade potato salad, vegetable salad, and some kind of baked blueberry dessert. Conversation came easily between them all, though having Maisie around kept it light, which suited Sage perfectly. Rowan didn't act strangely toward her, nor did he mention anything about what had happened between them, and she wondered if she had been the only one thinking about it for the past twenty-four hours.

"How long have you worked at the coffee shop?" Sage asked Delores as dessert wound down, but nobody had moved to get up from the table.

Delores's eyes sparkled when she answered. "Oh, I've worked there off and on over the years. Once I retired and my husband passed away, I found that I liked being there. There were always people around to talk with to keep my mind from dwelling on the loss of my Stuart." Her lips pulled into a small smile. "My friend Adam owns the place and he's been great with letting me work flexible hours so I can help Rowan with Maisie during the week."

Rowan's face held a grin of its own as he said to Sage, "Adam just likes having her around. She could probably stand at the counter and never do a minute's work and he'd still let her stay."

"Oh, Rowan, that's not true and you know it. He's a nice man and he's my friend. That's all." Sage couldn't miss the blush coloring Delores's cheeks.

"Whatever you say, Ma," Rowan teased and took a sip from his almost-empty water glass. He grinned at Sage.

The good-natured teasing between mother and son was sweet. Her own experience with family wasn't nearly as comfortable and relaxed as this little family seemed to be. Whereas Sage's family hardly ate together once she finished grade school, she had the distinct impression that these people sat and ate dinner together most nights.

"What about you?" Delores asked. "How is the work going on the house?"

Sage shared the projects she'd been working on, including the progress she'd been making upstairs and the developing thought of having a sliding door to the backyard installed in her bedroom.

"Are you still taking pictures?" Maisie said.

"I am," Sage said. "As a matter of fact, I took a bunch of pictures of the flowers that are blooming in my yard. And I'm glad you asked because I was wondering if you all know of any good scenic spots where I might take some more." The recent text she'd received from Millie, the owner of the gallery where she sold her work, had her thinking about photographing more of the area than just her house.

The Berkshires were a beautiful mix of rolling green hills and local ponds and hiking trails woven through dense green trees, and roads that meandered through little towns. She'd been so focused on her house, she'd neglected the natural environment all around her.

"I can go take pictures with you," Maisie said, hopping up onto her knees and leaning over the table toward Sage. "We can go tomorrow!"

"What?" Delores said. "You can't go take pictures tomorrow. You're supposed to help me watch Finn for Auntie."

"Oh," Maisie said, her lips pursed in a frown. "Can I take pictures with you another time?"

"Absolutely," Sage said. "I would love that."

Maisie's face beamed as she said to Sage, "My auntie has a baby and Gramma and I have to take care of him sometimes. I'm a really good babysitter."

"I'll bet you're the best at it and that your cousin loves when you babysit him," Sage said. Then to Rowan and Delores, "Does she live around here?"

"About twenty-five minutes from here," Delores said. "So, it's a decent drive, but not so far that we don't see them often." Her eyes softened. "I really wish she would move back here. It would be so much easier for me to watch the baby if she lived closer." She sighed then put her hands on the table and pushed herself to stand. "But it's out of my control," she said as she started to clear away the rest of the dinner dishes.

Being around this little family was nice. It was comfortable and easy. Being around Rowan when he was relaxed and laid-back only made him more attractive and more of a temptation to go against their agreement.

Rowan

Once the dishes were cleared and loaded into the dishwasher, Maisie asked if she could finally give Sage a tour of her bedroom. When Sage gave the thumbs up sign, Maisie grabbed her hand and pulled her toward the staircase. "Be nice to her, Zee," Rowan called behind them. "You don't want to scare her away!"

After a few minutes upstairs Rowan heard Sage saying all the right things, like, "Oh, that's pretty." And "Wow, so lovely." He imagined Maisie's face all but glowing from the compliments.

Walking to the bottom of the stairs, he called up. "All right, baby girl, it's time for you to get ready for bed. Why don't you send Miss Sage back down here." Maisie's exasperated sigh was audible even from downstairs. "I heard that," he teased. Maisie giggled. A minute or so later, the girls came back downstairs, Maisie with her pajamas in one hand, her other firmly grasping Sage's hand. Rowan's heart hitched at the sight. He'd never seen his daughter behave that way with anyone, except himself, his mother, and his sister.

"Thank you for showing me your room, Maisie," Sage said. "And thank you for inviting me over for dinner tonight. I had a lot of fun." She got down on one knee and pulled Maisie into a hug. "Thank you for being so nice to me since I moved here."

Ouch. He didn't know if that was a not-so-subtle dig at him for being a dick the first few times they interacted, but it sure felt like one. A well-deserved dig, but still a dig.

She stood back up and offered her thanks to his mother, who brushed it off. "Oh, sweetheart, you are welcome here any time at all. Thank you for being such wonderful company."

Sage picked up her purse and headed for the door, Rowan following directly behind her. "How about you let me walk you home?"

Her eyes sparkled and the hint of a smile pulled at her lips. "Are you sure you have time for that?"

"Time to walk you home? Yes," he said as they stepped through the door onto the porch. There was nothing he wanted more than to walk her home, follow her inside and fuck her until her voice was hoarse from screaming his name. "Time for anything else?" He sighed. "I wish."

The evening sky had darkened since Sage had arrived at the house. The dark clouds hung heavy and steely gray with water, looking as if they would burst open at any minute. Yet their steps were unhurried. They walked together as if they had the whole day to get back to her house. The easy conversation was interrupted a few times as thunder rumbled in the distance.

"I love a good summer thunderstorm," Sage said, standing still and looking up at the clouds, spreading her hands as if waiting for the rain to fall. "There's something romantic about them." Her long dark hair reached almost to her waist when she tipped her head back and Rowan stared at the delicate skin of her throat, wanting to press his lips against it. With a sigh, she lowered her arms and they started to walk again.

Their feet reached the walkway leading to Sage's house, and although neither said anything, they kept moving, strolling toward the end of the street. Rowan asked her about life in Boston, but she didn't really answer him. "Busy and loud," was all she said with a shrug of one shoulder.

"So, you don't miss it?" he asked.

She reached into her pocket and pulled out an elastic band that she used to pull her hair up into a ponytail. "Yes and no," she said. "I miss certain things, I guess. But others not as much." With a soft laugh she stared down at the sidewalk in front of her. "Wow, I don't think I could have been any vaguer if I tried, huh?"

Sage's ponytail showed off her long neck and Rowan followed its line of sight down to the front of her tank top where the line of her cleavage held his gaze. "If it's not something you want to talk about, it's not a big deal. There's plenty of other stuff in the world to talk about." He playfully bumped shoulders with her, and she flashed him a grin as they neared the end of the road.

"Which way?" she asked.

"That depends on how much time you want to spend with me."

"How about enough time for you to tell me what it was like growing up out here in the mountains," she said.

They took a right to continue the loop around the block as Rowan told her about life as a kid in Hazelton. "It was a great place to grow up. At least, as a little kid, it was. Lots of open space, places to play outside and ride bikes and stuff," he said. "As a teenager and young twenty-something it was a little less so, but it was still pretty good. You know the grocery store on the edge of town?"

"Yeah."

"Working there is sort of a rite of passage when you live here. I think every one of my friends worked there at some point in our lives."

"Did you work there?" she asked.

"It was my first job, and it was the first—and last—time I got fired from a job." He laughed at the dumbstruck look on her face.

"What? What did you do to get fired?"

Chuckling, he said, "I got caught making out with a girl I worked with in one of the walk-in refrigerators in the back of the store."

Sage burst out laughing. "You were making out inside a refrigerator?"

"In my defense, it was really hot outside and we had both gone into the walk-in to cool off. Except she had a crush on me and, well, I'm a guy, so..."

Sage smacked his arm playfully. "So, you were nice enough to kiss her to let her know what a nice guy you were?"

"That's pretty much how it happened." Rowan laughed at the memory of what an idiot he was. "You know, when you're seventeen, you don't always make the best choices."

"No," she said. "I suppose not." She was quiet for a few seconds then added, "Even in your twenties and thirties you don't always make the best choices."

It was a loaded statement. "That sounds like a story. Or two," he said.

Looking at him with a grin, she said, "It is, but for another day."

"Good enough."

They made a complete circle of the neighborhood and as they passed by his house again, the first fat drops of rain splashed down. Quickening their pace, they found themselves at the foot of the stairs to Sage's house. Her tank was polka-dotted with dark rain drops and a little rivulet of rain ran down the side of her face, almost daring Rowan to wipe it away.

He cleared his throat. "Thank you again for coming to dinner," he said. "You have no idea how happy you made my mother. Even though it's been almost six years since my dad passed, she still struggles without him. And having people over the house really makes her happy."

"No," she said. "Thank you, guys, for having me over. It was so much fun, and your mom is an amazing cook. So, really, tell her that anytime she wants to cook and invite me over, I'll be there."

Sage shuddered from the sudden coolness of the wind against her bare arms.

"I hate that I can't come inside with you," he said, hunching his shoulders against the the increasing rain as the wind whipped around them. "But I'm super late and I've gotta get Maisie to bed. She's got a big day of babysitting ahead of her tomorrow and she's super cranky when she's tired."

"I completely understand," she said. "I'll see you Sunday then. And thank your mom again for dinner." She hurried into the house and despite the cold heaviness of his drenched clothes, he waited for her to walk inside. A few seconds later the window curtain next to the front door fluttered open and Sage waved to him, then turned away, letting the curtain close behind her.

Sage

Despite the wildness of the storm the night before, Saturday dawned bright and beautiful. It promised to be a hot summer day and Sage was ready for it now that Rowan had installed the dedicated electric lines so she could put in a couple window air conditioner units.

Dressed in shorts and a ratty t-shirt, her hair pulled off her neck in a high ponytail, Sage worked to install the two units on the first floor before she moved to the guest room upstairs. Her mattress and bed frame had been ordered, and once they were delivered, she'd be moving her bedroom up there.

Once she had them all turned on and her house cooling down, she grabbed a cold glass of water and headed out to enjoy the warmth of the sunshine from her front porch, which was quickly becoming her favorite aspect of the house.

As she lifted the glass to her lips, Rowan's truck rolled down the street toward her house. She waited for him to drive by so she could wave, but rather than drive by, he pulled into her driveway and killed the ignition.

Jeans and a long-sleeved tee shirt had never looked better than they did on Rowan's body. Hopping to her feet, she met him at the bottom of the steps. "What are you doing here?" she asked. "I didn't think I'd be seeing you until Sunday."

He grinned as he leaned down to press his lips against hers. "Good morning to you too," he said.

Smiling, she wrapped her free arm around his waist, rested her head on his chest. "Good morning," she said. Then repeated herself. "So, for real, what are you doing here? Did you come to get some extra work done? Because you didn't need to."

Taking a step back from her, he looked her over from head to toe, a sexy grin pulling at his lips. "I'm not here to work," he said. "I'm here to take you and your camera up to Horsetail Falls."

"What's Horsetail Falls?" She smiled as Rowan reached for a few strands of hair that had broken free of her messy bun and wound them in a little circle on top of her head. They'd never stay where he put them, but the act was sweet, nonetheless.

Trailing his thumb down her cheek, he said, "It's one of the coolest places around here. There's a bunch of hiking trails and a really beautiful waterfall. Legend has it that it was named by a little girl who thought the water falling over the rocks at the top of the falls looked like a horse tail. Hence the name."

Looking down at her scrappy clothes she said, "Give me five minutes to change."

Half an hour later, Rowan pulled the truck into a small gravel parking area, the wheels crunching over the small stones as he drove to an empty space to park. The parking lot was entirely surrounded by trees and low shrubs, with only a few other cars parked there.

She placed her backpack on the ground when she stepped out of the truck, unzipped it to take out her camera. "Hold up," Rowan said. "Put it all back down and step over here." He indicated a spot about two feet in front of him, facing away from the cars. He shook a dark green can and popped off the bright orange cap. "OK, cover your face and stop breathing." She obeyed his instruction while he sprayed bug spray all over the front of her.

She yelped when the cold spray landed on her bare legs, and accidentally inhaled a mouthful. "Oh, my God," she gasped, then started coughing, trying to get the horrible taste from her mouth.

He reached into his own backpack and pulled out a bottle of water, unscrewed the cap, and handed it to her. "Here," he said. "Take a drink and spit it out."

Grateful he'd thought to bring water, she rinsed the bug spray from her mouth, at least as much as she could, and handed back the bottle.

"OK. Turn around," he said. After he sprayed the back side of her, she walked a few paces away before she took a deep breath then returned to spray him down.

Rowan stood before her, with his hands pressed to his face, his shirtsleeves straining against his biceps and Sage took an extra second to admire him. His shoulders were a sight unto themselves, but combine them with those arms, and a girl could spend some time getting used to touching them. His long legs were muscled, and his thighs looked like they'd be strong enough to hold her up while her legs wrapped around his waist.

"You gonna spray me or spend all day admiring me?" he said, peeking through his fingers. "Don't worry. I'll need you to get my back too, so there's more to see."

Sage shook the can and pretended she was going to spray it directly at his head. He quickly sucked in a gulp of air and closed his fingers over his face. "Your turn to turn around," she said after she had sprayed his front.

He wasn't kidding when he said there would be more to see when he turned around. With his hands up covering his face, Sage was able to appreciate more fully the broad expanse of a back that gave way to a narrow waist and a superb ass. She scolded herself internally. Rowan Kennedy was a guy, just like all the rest of them. *Casual. Keep things casual.*

After she doused him with the foul-smelling bug spray, he turned to her. "You get enough, or do you need to stare a little longer?" and he flashed that grin that she was dead set against falling for.

Ignoring him, she retrieved her backpack and hooked it over her shoulders. "I'm ready when you are."

Rowan led the way to a trail head marked with a sign that read, "Horsetail Falls 3/4 mile" with an arrow pointing up a well-worn path that was easily wide enough for both of them. As they walked on, they spoke in hushed tones, perhaps out of respect for the other hikers who may have been in the area, or perhaps in reverence of the quiet, tranquil mood of the nature that surrounded them. Whatever the reason, it felt right to keep their voices low.

They settled into a comfortable pace as the trail began its steady incline, each of them paying close attention to tree roots and smaller rocks, so as not to trip or turn an ankle. At one point they crossed a small wooden bridge that, according to Rowan, had been installed to protect the stream and wetland beneath it.

Excitement bubbled up in her and she asked to stop so she could take some photos. He was nice enough to hold her backpack while she gently stepped over and around rocks and plants in order to frame the perfect shots. "What made that?" she asked, pointing to an animal track in the mud.

Rowan crouched down to look. "Raccoon," he said.

She took several shots of the track from different angles, waited for the sun to sprinkle its rays around as the breeze blew the leaves overhead. When she was satisfied, she packed the camera away, hoisted up her backpack, and followed Rowan as he led the way to the waterfall. They climbed for about an hour, including all the time she stopped for more photos, neither saying much but with a sense of building possibility hanging heavy in the air between them.

The air took on a cool humidity from the spray of the crashing water. Layers of flat gray rock sandwiched atop one another formed a natural wall on one side of the falls, while ascending boulders formed a staircase of sorts, being overflowed by raging water from somewhere further up in the woods.

Sparkling sunlight glinted off the wet rocks and the churning pool at the base of the falls. "Rowan, this is stunning. It is so beautiful," she said, standing transfixed by the view in front of her. "It won't be difficult to get some good shots here." Her senses felt heightened, like she could hear every gurgle of water and see each and every fleck of sunshine. Despite the cool air, the sun continued to warm her skin as it shone through the canopy of leaves.

She squatted down to take her camera out again.

"Yeah, it's pretty nice," he said. "Maisie likes to come up here with me." He pointed to a couple picnic tables that Sage hadn't seen tucked in between some large tree trunks behind them. "We like to bring sandwiches and eat over there. When it's warm enough and the falls aren't raging, she likes when I take her down to put her feet in the water."

Looking where he pointed, she saw a small outcropping of boulders that she imagined would make a fun place from which to dip your toes in the water. She focused her camera on the area and snapped a few shots. Casting a glance back at Rowan, she said, "She is a really sweet girl."

"Thanks," he said. "I like her."

"She had so much fun putting together a little bouquet from my flower garden when she and your mom came to introduce themselves when I first moved in." She took a few photos of the enormous trees surrounding them. "She said they were for you. Did you ever get them?"

"I did. She put them in a glass on my bureau so I could see them when I woke up. They lasted a few days before the petals started to fall off." Something in Rowan's face softened as he said, "But she was more excited about meeting you than the flowers."

"Oh, my gosh, that's so sweet," she said, placing a hand over her heart, but unsure how to feel about his words. Getting seriously involved with Rowan would be entirely more complicated than any of the other guys she'd dated since he had a child to worry about. Not to mention she still had no idea what her future held.

"Have you decided what you're doing with the house once it's fixed up?" he asked, as if he'd been reading her mind. "You think you'll head back east, or will you stay out here?"

"I haven't decided yet," she said as she crouched down to take some close ups of the leaves, specifically the frilly ferns that grew low to the ground. "I still have a lot to do in the house before I can make any longer-term plans." Leaning over, she took a few shots of the water as it swirled in the basin. "Speaking of, do you think your friend would be available and interested in helping out with my bathrooms?"

Rowan had moved and stood leaning against a narrow, but tall, tree trunk, watching her work. "We're both working on the same build-out job across town so I can certainly ask him when I get back to work on Monday, unless you want me to ask him now."

"Nope, no rush," she said. "Don't mess up his weekend with work talk. Monday's fine." Raising her camera, she focused on Rowan leaning against the tree with his arms folded across his broad chest. He looked entirely natural standing there, and yet there was something that drew her to him. She liked looking at him and pressed the shutter button.

Rowan

Rowan's life had never been so busy. Work at the Faraway Inn took up his days, and after dinner, bath, and bedtime for Maisie, his evenings were spent at Sage's house. The electrical work had been mostly completed so he started showing up to help her with other things around the house. The second floor was completely done, and she was waiting for the furniture to be delivered.

Neither of them had brought up the idea of keeping things casual as whatever was beginning between them showed no signs of slowing down. Despite his promise to keep it professional when he showed up, invariably they ended up in bed together. Or up against a wall. Or in the shower. Or, his favorite position so far, driving into her from behind while she stood with her with her hands splayed against the wall.

By the time Saturday rolled around, he was more than ready for the cookout his mother had planned for no reason other than having her family all together for an afternoon. Maisie played on the swing set with Finn while Delores hovered nearby. Erin and Marcus flanked him at the grill while he cooked burgers and dogs for everyone.

"Sage coming over?" Marcus asked, taking a sip from his beer.

"Supposed to be. She's waiting for a delivery that's supposed to get there in the next hour or so and then she was planning to come down."

Erin looked from Marcus to Rowan. "Ah, yes. The mysterious Sage," she teased. "I heard all about her last weekend when Mom and Zee babysat Finn, but I have yet to meet her."

Rowan groaned. "Mom is in total matchmaker mode. I swear she'd have us married off it was up to her." He laughed and started flipping the burgers.

"It wasn't Mom," Erin said, eyeing him suspiciously. "It was Maisie. The girl didn't stop talking about her the whole time I was around." Her grin widened. "Seems it's not just Mom who's taken with your new girlfriend."

He'd known that since the day Sage rolled into town and Delores made it a point to work her into their lives. He was still embarrassed by the amount of time it took him to realize he'd fallen just as hard for her as his mother and daughter had. Harder in fact.

"It's pretty remarkable, actually," Marcus said to Erin. "Considering he wanted to toss her ass on the first bus out of town a month ago."

"Two questions," Erin said with a laugh. "First, why did you want to kick your girlfriend out of town? Second, is that food almost ready? I'm starving."

"One, I wanted her gone because she wasn't my girlfriend, she was a woman I hated because she bought my house," Rowan said as he flipped the burgers and dogs onto the waiting rolls. Handing his sister the tray, he said. "And two, here. Go eat."

Calling the kids to the table, Erin carried the tray away, while Marcus stayed behind. "How are things really going with you two? She get you to give up on your 'I want to stay single forever' bullshit yet?"

Rowan laughed, took a sip from the summer ale on the table beside him. "Fuck you."

Marcus's grin stretched across his whole face. "Come on, man, I'm serious. How's it going?"

Thinking of the fun they had together, not just their sexual compatibility, there was only one way to answer that. "Things are pretty good."

"Just pretty good?"

"At first, she told me she wanted to keep things strictly casual between us," Rowan said.

"And you agreed to that? Marcus said, his head snapping back slightly. Then he said, "I guess having non-solo sex for the first time in two years would make you agree to anything, huh?"

"You're a fucking dick, you know that?" Rowan said. Then in a whisper, he added, "And it was more like two and a half years."

"Damn," Marcus said, throwing a hand over Rowan's shoulder and howling in laughter, while Rowan stared him dead in the eye. "I'm sorry, dude, really," Marcus said as his laughter died away.

"Anyway," Rowan continued. "She hasn't really brought it up again and things have been anything but casual between us."

"That's great, man, really," Marcus said. "I'm glad to hear you're coming out of your shell and trying to make something happen with her." He clapped Rowan on the shoulder. "I'm happy for you."

"Thanks, bud, I appreciate that," Rowan said.

"How's the renovation stuff going over there?" Marcus asked as they walked to the table to grab some lunch.

"It's good," he said. "She's doing a ton of work on the place, and it looks a hundred times better than it did, that's for sure."

"But?"

Rowan slid onto the bench next to Maisie and Marcus sat across from him, next to Erin.

"Are you not into the changes she's making?" Marcus said.

All adult eyes at the table turned to him and he wished they would go back to eating their lunch instead of openly eavesdropping on his conversation. "You know how it is. It's her house so she's painting and decorating and all that stuff the way she wants to. It's not exactly the way I would've done it but what are you gonna do?" He bit off a mouthful of burger and chewed. "Oh, that reminds me," he said after he swallowed down his bite of burger. "Sage wanted me to ask if you'd be interested and available to do the work in the bathrooms over there?"

"Yeah, sure. Let me check the schedule and I'll let you know."

The screen door on the side of the house clanked shut and all eyes turned to see Sage walking out with a bowl in one hand and a beer in the other. His heart hitched as she came out to the lawn to join the family lunch.

His mother and his daughter were equally quick to call out to her while Erin looked from Sage to Rowan and smiled. "She's pretty," Erin whispered.

"Hi, honey," Delores said, waving Sage closer. "Come on over and let me introduce you to everyone."

If he was more sure of her comfort level, he would have stood and given her a kiss as she walked over but she already gave off the slight air of discomfort with everyone staring at her. Instead, he waited for Delores to introduce Marcus and Erin and Finn then stood to make room for her on the bench. Her hand on his shoulder told him she appreciated the low-key approach.

"Did your delivery get there OK?" Rowan asked as she tucked into a burger and some baked beans.

"Mm," she said, wiping a spot of ketchup from her lips. "They dropped everything off a little while ago and I came right over as soon as they left."

"Can I come see the stuff you got?" Maisie asked from several seats away.

"Of course you can," Sage said. "And speaking of all that stuff," she said with exaggerated excitement for Maisie's benefit. "I still have to buy a bunch more stuff to decorate the guest room and I was hoping you'd want to come with me?"

Maisie's entire body bounced on the bench, and she looked directly at Rowan. "Can I, Daddy? Can I go with Miss Sage to buy stuff?"

"Uh..." He looked at Sage. "When are you going?"

"I was thinking about tomorrow morning. Maybe around ten or so."

"Can I go, Daddy? Please! I want to go," Maisie yelled.

"Easy, honey," Delores said, moving Maisie's drink out of spilling range.

Erin smiled at Maisie while Marcus ignored it all and kept shoving food in his mouth.

"Sounds alright with me," Rowan finally said.

"Yay!"

Sage

T he nearest mall was a twenty-minute drive, so Rowan had in-
    stalled Maisie's car seat in Sage's Prius. After buckling Maisie
into the back seat he pulled Sage into his arms and said, "Are you sure
you want to do this? You really don't have to."

Sage peeked over his shoulder to see Maisie in her seat waiting
patiently, then said to Rowan, "Yes, I do. What kind of jerk would I
be to renege on my offer after she's already in the car?" Rowan's smile
warmed her as much as his hands holding onto her waist did.

In a very short time she had come to appreciate those hands and
what they were capable of, both in the bedroom as well as out of it. He
was a hard worker, a great dad, a dutiful son, a generous lover. When
he pressed his lips to hers one last time before she left, Sage closed her
eyes and breathed him in, craving the way he was invading every cell of
her body, yet unsteady in the knowledge of whether she was making
the right decision by letting him get close.

If only he hadn't mentioned the house at the cookout. She had been
standing in Delores's kitchen with her hand on the doorknob when

she heard him tell Marcus he didn't like all the things she'd been doing there but it was still OK. It should have been a throwaway statement about differing decorating choices, but it wasn't. There was something else behind those words, something deeper.

Over the past two months she had let herself get close to him, close to his family. Armed with a newfound apprehension, she started to second guess her judgment. Her ability to choose wisely had taken a hit over the last couple years, starting with Joe and ending with already-married Drew.

Her head reeled with so many thoughts, she was glad for the moment Rowan finally released her, waved at Maisie through the window. "Behave yourself today," he said. "You make sure you listen to Sage the same way you listen to me. Got it?"

"Got it," she said. "I'll listen even better to Sage," she promised in her sweet little girl voice, tracing a little x over her heart. "Bye, Daddy!"

"Of course you will," he muttered under his breath, then after one last wave to Maisie, Rowan smiled at Sage and hopped into his truck. "Shoot me a text if you need anything. I've just got to run out and grab a few things for work tomorrow, I won't be gone long." He cast a glance out his back window and said, "And my mother should be home all morning too, if you need her."

"We'll be fine," Sage assured him. "Now, can you move your truck so we can go do some shopping?"

"Yes, ma'am," he said and pulled out of the driveway with a wave.

#####

Inside the bed and bath store, Maisie's eyes popped open so wide Sage teased her that they were going to fall out. Clearly Rowan was not a regular in that store. "It's so big in here," she said. "What stuff are you gonna buy?" Her head swiveled from one side of the store to the other and then stopped at the As Seen on TV display right in front of her face. "Hey! I've seen this on the commercials when Gramma watches her shows," she said as she picked up a fry pan with a picture of a fried egg taped to the inside. "Do you think they really work that good?"

Sage shrugged. "Don't know. Never used one. But if I do, I'll let you know." She reached out and Maisie held her hand as easily as if they'd been doing it every day for years. The warmth of her little hand in Sage's tore a little harder at her heart as she listened to the voice inside her that told her she was making a mistake. Again. That there was something going on that Rowan wasn't telling her. "Come on," she said. "The sheets and stuff are around the back of the store, I think."

They walked hand-in-hand past a kitchen section with an assortment of gadgets and cookware sets and spice racks that left Sage's head reeling. Maisie had questions about everything they passed. "What do you do with that?" she asked about a pan rack. "What are those for?" she said, pointing to a spice carousel. "That's for coffee," she said when she saw a countertop coffee grinder. "Daddy has one of those. It's really loud, though. I hate it."

Sage couldn't have answered all of Maisie's questions because she had already moved on to another interest-catching display before Sage had time to respond. The speed with which she pivoted from one thing to the next had Sage exhausted before they even made it out of the kitchen department.

With a gentle tug she led Maisie around the corner and watched her eyes grow huge all over again at the endless shelves of bedding. Maisie dropped Sage's hand and ran to a display that had been done up in bright yellows and greens with some white accent pieces.

"You like this one?" Sage asked. "You think it would look good in my guest room?"

Maisie blinked and then refocused on Sage. A little hint of sadness flitted across her face before it was replaced by pure adoration. "I love this," she said lying down with her arms outstretched, hugging the bed. "It's so beautiful."

"Oh," Sage said. "You like this for your own room, you mean?"

Maisie nodded, though she was still lying on the bed. "Gramma bought my one I have now, but she likes pink."

"That's right," Sage said. "You like yellow."

"Yeah." Maisie sighed.

Sage didn't want Maisie getting bogged down being sad over a bedding set, so she said, "The guest room in my house is more set up for colors like dark green and beige, maybe a touch of pale yellow." She reached down to take hold of Maisie's hand again. "Think you can help me find a set like that? I need sheets and pillows and a comforter and curtains and a throw rug and some hangers and a garbage basket."

Maisie's head lifted from the yellow bed, and she took Sage's hand. "That's a lot of stuff for one room."

"Not really. Don't you have all that stuff in your room?"

Maisie tilted her head to the side, thinking about her bedroom, then nodded. "I do have all that stuff!" she said. "It's just all pink."

They moved around the bedding department, trying to find a set that fit what Sage had in mind for the guest room. It didn't take long before Maisie spotted an ensemble that would fit perfectly. "That's exactly what I was looking for. Nice job finding that for me." Maisie's cheeks practically split in a huge smile in response to Sage's praise. "Can you help me find a sheet set that says K on it for king size?" They looked together for a few seconds while Sage waited for Maisie to find the right letter. "Awesome," Sage said and held up her hand for a fist bump. Maisie giggled and her infectious smile had Sage smiling right back.

"Hey, Sage," Maisie whispered. Pulling her hand, Maisie tugged Sage down to be at her own eye-level. Squatting down to hear what Maisie had to say, Sage wasn't prepared when the girl leaned over, pushed Sage's hair out of the way and whispered, "Can you be my mom?"

Sage's heart all but shattered in her chest as the sweet little girl before her held her gaze with the most earnest eyes she'd ever seen. Sage had no idea how to answer her. Mind reeling, she reached out and pulled Maisie in for a hug and the little one wrapped her arms around Sage's neck.

Words battled in her mind and in her heart and finally came together in a way she hoped would be acceptable to Maisie. "How about this?" Sage said, moving her to arm's length and looking her in the eye. "How about for this whole day I can totally pretend to be your mom. What do you think?"

Maisie's eyes grew round, and she nodded. For a split-second Sage thought Maisie was going to cry, but then surprised her by saying, "Yay! And do you know what?"

"What?"

"Can you come to my birthday party?"

Laughing at the abrupt shift, Sage said, "You're having a birthday party?"

"Yeah, at Gramma's house and my friends are all coming, and my daddy and my uncle Marcus are going to make hamburgers and my Auntie Erin, and my cousin Finn are coming too!"

"Oh my gosh, Maisie, that sounds amazing. I can't wait to go. Do you know when it is?"

"Next Saturday."

Rowan hadn't mentioned anything about a party, and she hoped she wasn't overstepping their 'casual' agreement, though things between them had blown way past casual weeks ago. "I am ninety-nine percent sure I can go but I'll let you know for sure later, alright?"

"OK," Maisie said then leaned down to pick up the set of sheets from the floor.

Sage grabbed the comforter set under one arm and they picked out four sets of matching curtains and four new pillows before she said, "I think we need a shopping cart."

They wrangled all their items into a blue plastic cart then walked around again to find some of the things Sage needed to complete the room. She grabbed a small trashcan and put it in the cart. Maisie found a perfect makeup mirror that would work nicely up there in the evenings when the yellow overhead lights were no good for putting on makeup.

"Hey, Sage?"

"What's up?"

"Did you do the sex with my dad?"

Sage crashed the shopping cart into a display full of shower curtain rings, sending boxes skittering across the floor. "Oh crap," she said as she stooped to gather up the runaway rings. Then she looked at Maisie, who stood with a couple boxes of shower curtain rings in her hands and a look of utter confusion on her face. "What even is that?" Maisie said.

"First, that's a question for your dad," Sage said, shoving a couple of escaped rings into boxes. "Not me. And second, why did you ask me about it, if you don't mind telling me?"

Maisie hung the plastic boxes on the pegs of the display. "I heard Uncle Marcus say it the other day. He asked my dad if he did the sex, and my dad said some bad words." She giggled and Sage couldn't help but smile with her. "But that's OK because he had to put two dollars into the swear jar." She paused, looking at Sage. "So, did you?"

Sage wondered if all kids were that curious and full of questions, or if the universe just happened to put this one in her life to shake things up. Her first instinct was to admit it, but she worried that was out of line with a five-year-old, but what the hell did she know of little kids? She had no siblings. Her cousins were both close to her in age, so when they were little, she was too. Was this the kind of thing all kids asked? Would it be OK to brush her off, or redirect her toward something else? What would Rowan think of her answer either way? Where the hell was Rowan and why wasn't he there to field this one?

"You know, Maisie, those aren't really questions I can answer for you. I don't think it would be appropriate for me to do so. I think you'd better talk to your dad if you have questions like that." She hoped that was the right thing to say and that Maisie wouldn't throw some kind of tantrum or whatever kids did when they were pissed off.

Maisie shrugged. "OK," she said and turned her attention to a bin of potpourri packets. She picked one up, held it to her nose and inhaled a deep breath. "Hey, these would smell nice in that bedroom."

Rowan

Maisie hadn't stopped talking about Sage and how much fun they had since Sage brought her home earlier in the day. His intention had been to visit Sage that evening by himself but Delores was out on a date with her friend Adam and most likely wouldn't be home until tomorrow, so he had no choice but to bring Maisie with him.

It seemed Sage was taking advantage of the warm summer evening by leaving her front door open. Looking at her through the screen door for an extra second, he took in the scene before him. Her hair hung loose down her back, framing her face. Wearing her normal outfit of yoga pants and a tee shirt, she was sitting with her feet tucked beneath her, folding laundry. In short, she was stunning. He rapped his knuckle lightly on the door.

"Come on in," she called. Her face lit up as soon as she made eye contact with him. Pushing the laundry to the side, she stood to greet them. He wanted to reach out and pull her into his arms, but Maisie beat him to it by sprinting across the room and jumping into her arms first.

"Hey, sweetheart," Sage said, setting Maisie's feet on the floor. "Thank you for coming back with your dad to help me tonight."

Now that he was fully inside the house, the stacks of boxes and mountain of shopping bags came into full view. "Where did that all come from?" he asked. "Did you two buy all of that today?"

Still holding Maisie's hand, she came over to stand beside him in front of the giant pile. "Some of it was delivered yesterday but, yeah," she said, looking down on Maisie. "The rest was all stuff we bought today. Can't very well live in a house with nothing in it, right?"

Maisie's head shook so fast her whole body wobbled with the effort.

Having no idea what was in any of the bags, he couldn't begin to add up the money she'd spent but he was willing to bet it wasn't a small amount. Several lamps were tucked in between huge shopping bags filled with pillows and, he guessed, lots of sheets and towels, not to mention the boxes of plates and dishes and glassware. Appliances of all sorts peeked from the tops of several bags, including a stand mixer. Did Sage even cook? "How much did you drop on all of this?"

Her smile evaporated. "I don't know. What's the difference? It was all stuff I needed so I had to get it." She playfully tugged Maisie's hand and looked at her with round eyes. "Wanna help me carry this stuff upstairs and help me set it up?"

Maisie jumped up and down, shaking Sage's whole arm. "Yes!" She quickly looked at him. "I'm gonna help Miss Sage, OK, Daddy?"

"Absolutely, baby girl." He reached down and picked up a couple of bed pillows, handed them to her. "Why don't you start with this?" She took off running and Rowan yelled, "Walk up the stairs, please. I don't want you getting hurt."

"Help me with this one?" Sage said, pointing at a large flat box with her toe. "It's the frame for the day bed I'm putting in the guest room. The mattresses will be here Wednesday and then I can move upstairs and start the work in my bedroom." She flashed a goofy, excited grin as she bounced on her toes.

"I don't know who's more excited about all this stuff, you or Maisie," he said with a laugh, then reached down to help carry the bed frame.

Over the next hour, he and Sage carried the rest of the furniture boxes up the stairs while Maisie helped by holding doors and carrying the lighter bags from the pile.

By the time they were done carrying everything up, Maisie flopped onto the floor with her limbs out in every direction. "Watch out, Zee. Sage and I need to get this bed put together." He tried shooing her out of the way, but she grunted her frustration at him. "Hey," he said, his tone sharper than before. "I need you to move so we can put this bed together, please."

Her slow blinks and extended yawns told him he was on borrowed time before a meltdown hit. "How about I bring you home and then I'll come back and help Miss Sage in a little while?"

"No," she said, slapping her hands on the floor. "I want to stay here with you and help."

"I think it's best if we go home, Zee," he said.

"No," she said again, firmer this time. Then she looked him in the eye and realization dawned that she may have gone too far, and her little chin started to wobble.

He pushed out a harsh breath and took a step toward her, ready to pick her up and carry her back to their house. Before he could reach her, she scrambled to her feet, grabbed a pillow from the stack of bedding, and clutching it to her little body, stomped down the length of the hallway into Sage's new office.

For such a small human she had an awfully big personality. Sage tried hiding her smile behind her hand.

He quickly turned to her and closed the distance between them, hauling her into his arms while he pushed her back against the wall. "Something funny?" he said, pulling his face into a frown and placing his hands on either side of her head, trapping her where she stood.

She opened her mouth to respond but he angled his mouth to hers, muffling whatever words she was trying to say. Eventually she gave up talking and eased into his kiss, curling her fingers up into his hair and holding his body close. She sighed, a contented sound, and his dick responded like it had been trained to stand at attention at her slightest call.

Giving in to his body's reaction to her, he pressed his hips forward, leaned his forehead against hers. "See what you do to me?" he said as she tilted her head to look him in the eye. "What am I supposed to do with this now?" He angled his hips a little deeper and she inhaled a sharp breath.

"Don't blame me for that," she teased. "It was you who kissed me, remember?"

"I remember," he said, lowering his hands from the wall to her shoulders. He leaned in for another kiss and let his fingers trail down the front of her, waiting for her nipples to respond to his touch.

She tried to break free of his hands and his mouth, mumbling something about "the next room."

"She'll be asleep in five minutes, if she isn't already," he said, not letting Sage retreat from her place between his arms. "You'll just have to be really quiet," he whispered against the shell of her ear.

Her eyes bugged out. "You're kidding me, right?"

"Do I look like I'm joking?" He turned them as one and walked her backwards toward the open closet. She threw her arms around his neck, and hoisting her off the floor, he carried her inside the empty closet. Setting her feet on the ground he spun her to face the wall, reached his hands around and yanked her pants down to her knees.

"Rowan," she whispered.

In a flash, he freed himself from his pants, pushed her forward so her hands were splayed against the wall, lined up at her entrance and drove into her hard. She clamped one hand over her mouth to stifle her cry. "Hands on the wall," he ordered as he pumped into her, so slick and hot for him. Whimpering, she pressed her hands back where he wanted them.

With one hand he grabbed her hip, the other he slid around front and between her legs. Sage's head lolled back with a soft moan, and he pressed his cheek against hers, never letting up the pressure between her thighs or the steady rhythm of his hips.

Her breathing turned to panting and Rowan knew she was close. "Shh," he whispered in her ear. "You have to be quiet."

She nodded her understanding, her body shaking with ragged breaths.

Inhaling sharply, her legs trembled beneath her, fingers twitching and clawing at the wall. She was working hard to rein in the cries her body was begging her to let loose. Rowan wrapped his arms around her waist to keep her standing as he drove into her over and over until he released inside her with a choked grunt.

They stayed still in the closet, his arms fastened around her, and she leaned her head back against his shoulder while he traced his fingers up and over her slender throat, peppering kisses along her cheek and jaw.

"Holy shit," she whispered. "Was I quiet enough? Because that was the hardest thing I've ever done." Her body shook with quiet laughter.

He squeezed her and whispered against her ear, "You were perfect. Absolutely fucking perfect."

A tear splashed down on his forearm.

Quickly putting himself back together, he reached down and helped her put her clothing to rights. "Oh, my God, what's the matter? Why are you crying? Did I hurt you?" What a fucking dick thing to do, just plow into her with no warmup. Of course he hurt her.

He turned her around and his heart struck his ribs at the sight of her glossy eyes and trembling lip. "I am so, so sorry," he said and leaned down to kiss the tears from one cheek while he wiped the other with the pad of his thumb.

She breathed out a laugh through her tears and wiped away the ones that remained, pushing the heels of her hands into her eyes. "You didn't hurt me." She dropped eye contact and looked at his chest. "I kinda thought that part was obvious," she teased then looked back to meet his eyes.

"What's wrong then?"

Looking around the small space, she said, "I'm not sure, to tell you the truth." Rowan wasn't the best at understanding women, but he was fairly certain she wasn't telling the truth.

He held her body close to his own and kissed the top of her head. "You'd tell me if it was something I did, right?" Her face rubbed against his chest as she nodded under his chin.

"What are you doing in there?" Maisie's voice asked from right behind him.

Sage jumped, her head cracking into his jaw, sending an electric bolt of pain through his head. "Fuck!" he yelled. Spinning around, holding his aching jaw in one hand, he came face to face with his daughter, who stood with heavy-lidded eyes and a ponytail that was hanging on by its last leg.

"Are we going home soon?" she asked.

"Hey, baby girl," Rowan said, nearly choking on his heart which sat firmly lodged in his throat. Miss Sage and I were just talking a minute. She's kinda sad and she needed a little privacy, that's all."

His heart pounded in his chest at the realization of the stupid mistake he had made dragging Sage into the closet. He couldn't even think about how this would have played out if Maisie had woken up three minutes earlier. Running his hand through his hair, he looked down at her with a tenderness that only she evoked.

"Is she OK?" Maisie said, trying to peek around him to get a look at Sage. "Does she need a hug?" Her little heart was so kind and gentle. Her eyes held a sincerity that he couldn't figure out. He knew it couldn't have come from himself, and it sure as hell didn't come from her missing-in-action mother.

"I'm OK, Maisie," Sage said. "But I can always use a hug." When she stepped out from behind him, Maisie scurried past to jump into her arms.

Now all he had to do was figure out why the hell Sage's laughter turned to crying after they finished having sex. That couldn't have been a good omen.

Sage

"Give us a few seconds, Zee, OK?" Rowan asked. "Can you wait for me down by the front door and I'll be there in one minute?"

With one last, heartfelt look at Sage, Maisie retreated from the closet and walked out of the room.

"I am so sorry," he said again. "I never should have done that."

Why did things have to be so complicated? What did her house have to do with any of it? Why couldn't she come right out and ask him what he was hiding from her? Because she was afraid of what the answer would be. Maybe not in words, but in the moment of truth that often gave people up as it flashed across their faces. And her heart was not prepared for that.

"Let's just be glad it was quick instead of being sorry it happened," she teased.

A smile pulled at one side of his mouth and cradling her face, he ran one thumb across her cheek. "Come back to my place with me?" he said.

Looking at the solid wall of his chest instead of his face, she said, "I don't know if that's a good idea." It would certainly be best for her heart to keep her distance from him, but her body was another story. The more time she spent with him, the more she wanted to be near him.

"I think it's a good idea if we talk but I've got to get her home to bed." Tipping her chin to look eye-to-eye with her, he said, "Please? Even for an hour or so and you can come right back if you want."

Forty minutes later, after Rowan had taken Maisie home and Sage had taken a quick shower, she approached the front porch of the big white farmhouse. Rowan sat on the porch swing, beer in hand with another on the small table beside him.

He handed one to her as he made room for her on the swing. "Thank you," she said and took a sip. The cool liquid felt good after the busy day she'd had. "That's nice. Hits the spot, even."

Rowan was quiet beside her. "Thank you," he finally said. "For today. With Maisie."

"What about today? I should be thanking you for letting me take Maisie with me." She took another sip. "It was nice having a shopping buddy."

He put his bottle down beside the swing and reached his arm around her back, pulling Sage close. "Thank you for being so amazing with her." He shook his head, emotion stopping whatever words he was about to say. Swallowing first, he said, "She told me about asking you to be her mom."

"Oh, Rowan, it was no big deal. Really," Sage said, hoping he wouldn't make it out to be more than it was.

"When she told me, I have to admit, I panicked. Like total fucking panic. I wanted to jump in and save the day and protect her and at the same time it had already happened and however you responded was already in the past. There was no way to protect her." He lifted his eyes to meet hers. "But you? You said the exact right thing at the exact right time. And you made her entire day." He was quiet again for a few seconds. "Thank you."

She blew out a relieved breath and threaded her fingers between his. "You're welcome. I'd be lying if I said I didn't panic when she asked, but I didn't know what else to say. I'm just glad it worked out as well as it did." She squeezed his fingers. "She really is a sweet girl. It's easy to be nice to her." Sage smiled at him, hoping to ease some of whatever emotional burden he was carrying, even for a few minutes.

"Can I kiss you?"

She nodded and Rowan inclined his head to hers, took her mouth with his own as he turned to face her. He moved his hand to pull stray hairs away from her neck and brush them down her back. His other hand still sat entwined with hers on her lap. Sage welcomed his tongue as it swept into her mouth and met her own. Her back relaxed as he leaned against her, his kiss becoming deeper, more intense.

Part of her brain bristled at the fact that they were making out on his mother's front porch. Then his hands on her body brought out a small moan as she surrendered to the moment, letting her thoughts float away and giving herself entirely to the pleasure of being the object of Rowan's affection.

As his tongue darted into her mouth and back out, she did the same to him, chasing him, begging him to come back, a request which he obliged over and over again. She raised her hands to run her fingers through his hair, holding his face, telling him silently how much she wanted him to keep kissing her, how much she liked having his tongue in her mouth.

Eventually she tipped her head back and he trailed kisses down her neck and across the skin just above the collar of her shirt. "Thank you for letting me kiss you," he said against her throat before he returned to sitting upright, resting his hand on her thigh as she leaned over and rested against his shoulder.

"Can I ask you something?" he said, pulling her out of her cozy thoughts.

"Of course, what's up?"

"Why did you move out here?" His tone was neutral, but his gaze stayed fixed on something in the foreground.

"I told you," she said. "My friend, Julia, is a real estate agent. One night we went out for dinner and drinks, and we started talking about the idea of me buying a vacation place out this way and one thing led to another and here I am."

Still staring straight ahead he nodded. "Yeah. I remember that much. But I mean why are you here?"

The evening breeze started to chill Sage's exposed skin. She rubbed her arms to keep away the goosebumps that had broken out all over her body. To share his body heat, she snuggled herself deeper into Rowan's side until he lifted his arm, and pulled her close. His fingers ran lazy strokes up her arm, and she felt the thrill of his touch throughout her entire body. "You're cold," he said. "Come on, let's get you inside."

"It's so nice out here. I hate to go in and miss this."

"Then let's go in and get you a sweatshirt or something to keep you warm." She nodded and he led the way through the door and upstairs to his bedroom. He peeked his head into Maisie's room as they quietly passed her door. "She's completely out. I swear that girl could sleep through a war." He laughed and took Sage's hand as they continued toward his bedroom, down the hall and on the opposite side from Maisie's.

Rowan's room looked like it belonged in a catalog. The wall behind his bed was paneled in distressed planks, exquisitely highlighting the king size bed with its wrought iron rail head and foot boards. The gray and white striped comforter brought out the deep gray accents in the rug that ran underneath the bed and extended a couple feet all around it. A tall bureau stood against the far wall and a matching low bureau with a large, attached mirror sat directly opposite his bed. She noticed a doorway on the near wall and guessed from the black and white checkered tiled floor that it was his bathroom.

"Rowan, this is amazing. You realize this looks like a guest room in a B&B, not just like a regular old bedroom, right?" She was afraid to touch anything for fear of spoiling the illusion. He opened his closet and pulled out a sweatshirt for her. Before she put it on, she held it to her face and inhaled his scent.

She thought she had been subtle.

"Did you just smell my sweatshirt?" he asked.

She hadn't been nearly subtle enough.

"Maybe," she said, dragging out the word while he grinned at her. "I like the way you smell, and I couldn't help myself," she finally said.

Rowan reached out and took the sweatshirt back from her, stepped closer and wrapped his arms around her back, letting his hands slide down and over her bottom, then giving it a good squeeze. "You have a great ass, did you know that?" he said into the crook of her neck as he bit her skin in little bites, sending a flood of heat through her body.

He trailed his fingers around the waist of her jeans until they had successfully undone the button. Sage reached her arms up and wrapped them around his neck while he slowly lowered the zipper and slid his hands inside her panties until he found what he was looking for.

Gasping, her head fell back as he deftly slid one finger along her center and pressed it slightly against her aching clit. "I love when you make that noise," he murmured against her ear. Slowly and deliberately he stroked her, easing into her and back out, over and over.

Her breaths came out in soft moans as she pushed her hips into his hand and felt the lack of him when he took his hand out of her panties. "I could listen to you all day," he said, bringing his hands to the hem of her shirt, lifting it straight up and over her head, then pushing her jeans to the floor, leaving her standing in a black lace bra and panties.

Hurrying to get him as undressed as she was, she ripped his shirt over his head and grabbed at his pants. Rowan stepped back, dragged his eyes over her, unhooked her bra, and watched it fall to the floor. Smiling appreciatively, he picked her up and carried her to his bed where he laid her down.

Rowan

Rowan could spend days, years, worshiping her body. As she lay before him, open, accepting, he had to stop and just look at her, take her in with his eyes, burn her into his memory. Her dark hair circled her head like a halo, her pink nipples peaked and waiting to be sucked, her hips already beginning to writhe in anticipation of joining with him.

Lying next to her, he reached one hand across to massage the far breast while he lowered his mouth to the near one. Sage's back arched into him as he drew her nipple into his mouth, swirled his tongue, and sucked. He gently squeezed and pinched her other nipple and was rewarded by a deep moan.

He rolled his body on top of hers, but not to penetrate her, not yet. Leaving her panties on, he lowered his mouth to the breast he had not yet tasted, gently pinching the other nipple. His dick twitched in response to her movements, her moaning breaths.

Kissing his way down her body, over her ribs and her belly, he massaged every bit of skin he touched, returning as often as possible to one breast or the other to lick and to suck. He flicked one nipple with his tongue, slowly at first, then quickly before he sucked it hard. With a gasp, she pressed her hips into him as he repeated the gesture on the other breast.

Her hips began to thrust, pushing against his erection while he continued to suck her nipples. She fluttered her hands against the tops of his shoulders as her body trembled beneath his. A high-pitched whimper followed by a shuddering groan of satisfaction escaped her lips. He studied her face as one sound melded into the next, her eyes tightly closed, a look bordering on pain that gave way quickly to one of relaxed satisfaction. It was the first time Rowan had given a woman a nipple orgasm, and it was so fucking hot there's no way it would be the last.

She was perfection. Her face, her body, her skin. Rowan shifted himself down her body again, this time he kissed his way from her breasts down the center of her chest, over her belly and down to the top of her panties. Her hands rested lightly on his back, and she occasionally reached up and twined her fingers into his hair.

"Move up higher on the bed," he said, his cheek pressed against the inside of her thigh so that his words vibrated through her center. Without a word she obeyed his instruction. Lowering his face between her legs, he placed tender kisses over the black lace before sliding one finger underneath, feeling how wet she was for him. It was a heady feeling, knowing that she wanted him just as badly as he wanted her, but this night promised only good things and there was no way he would rush it.

After pushing the fabric to the side, Rowan slid one finger along her center again, then raised his eyes to hers. "Look at me, Sage," he said. "Open your eyes and look at me." When her eyes fluttered open, her intense gaze found his and held it while he slid his finger deep inside her. Gasping, she closed her eyes again. "Uh-uh," he said, withdrawing his finger. "I said look at me." Again, she did as she was asked. "I want you to keep looking at me, Sage. If I see you close your eyes, I'm going to stop what I'm doing." A look of pain flashed across her face, and he knew he hit his target. She was loving this game as much as he was. "Do you understand?" he asked.

She nodded.

"I want to hear you say it," he said as he eased his finger into her again then withdrew it to make his point.

"I understand."

"Tell me what you understand, and I'll give it back to you."

The pained look flashed across her face again as she said, "I understand that If I stop watching you, you'll stop fingering me."

Her words, her tone of voice, and the look in her eyes combined to set off fireworks in his brain and he had to will himself not to come right then and there. "Good girl," he murmured and slipped his finger back inside her. "Is this what you want from me?" He held her gaze and continued sliding his finger into her. When she nodded, he added a second finger. "How about this?" he asked.

She was having trouble keeping her eyes focused on him instead of falling closed, but she managed to do it. "Yes," she said. "I like that." As he fingered her, her hips rocked against his hand. The expression on her face changed from pain to ecstasy, to desperation and need as he continued.

Pulling her bottom lip between her teeth, she bit down as her breaths turned into expectant grunts. She was close to coming and he was ready for it. He picked up his speed to match hers, then lowered his face and sucked her until she screamed, her body bucking beneath him, legs shaking with the force of her second orgasm.

"I'm sorry," she said, throwing her hands up over her face.

Rowan eased his fingers out, letting her body rest before he took it for his own release. "Sorry for what? That was fucking awesome," he said.

Hiding her face behind her hands, she said, "I didn't mean to scream. That was so loud. I am so, so sorry."

He kissed her inner thigh, sucking gently on the skin. "You were perfect, Sage. Don't ever say sorry for that."

Her hands fell away from her face, causing her breasts to bounce and Rowan's hard on to twitch in direct response. In a flash, he stood at the side of the bed, kicked his boxers to the floor, flipped Sage onto her belly and hauled her down so she was bent over the bed in front of him. With a firm grip on her hips, he lined himself up and drove himself into her with a grunt.

The blankets and mattress stifled the noises she made as he rocked into her, slowly at first, then with greater urgency. "That's it, Sage. Keep taking me deep," he said. "I want to feel you come again for me." Her whimpering picked up and she smothered her own sounds by pushing her face into the bed as he pounded into her again and again. "Come for me, Sage. Come hard for me," he ground out as he landed a hard smack on her ass cheek.

This time when she screamed, the sound was muffled by the blankets she had balled up under her face, but her legs still shook as she clenched around him. He couldn't have held back for anything at that moment of exquisite bliss, when nothing else existed aside from their connected bodies. Closing his eyes, he let the tingling in his body and the tightening in his balls reach their peak sensation as he finally released and came inside her with a punishingly deep thrust and an animalistic groan that shook him to his core.

With zero fucks to give about not staying casual, he had gone and fallen for the woman who lie, satiated and exhausted, beneath him.

Sage

F alling asleep tucked into Rowan's strong body, her breathing slowed to match his as they drifted off together more than two hours after they went to his room to get her a sweatshirt. Her intention had not been to stay the night, but after the soul-shaking sex and long, soaking shower, she had been exhausted enough that he'd easily convinced her to stay with him.

He fell asleep tracing little circles on her upper back and shoulders, sending the occasional shiver down her spine. Eventually she gave in to the pull of sleep and moved her head from his chest to her own pillow.

At some point in the middle of the night, her eyes popped open in a panic, not recognizing anything around her. Hearing Rowan's soft breathing beside her, she quickly remembered where she was and how she got there.

Holding the covers against her chest, she waited for her eyes to adjust to the darkness, then slid her feet to the floor and started rooting around the pile of clothes to find something to put on. She held up a tee shirt that clearly belonged to Rowan, but at the moment it didn't make any difference. She needed to be covered. Grabbing a pair of his sweatpants, she yanked them up her legs. As soon as she let them go, they slipped down past her ass and she hiked them again, cinching the drawstring to hold them up.

"Sage? Baby, what are you doing?" Rowan's voice was sleepy. "You don't need to get dressed, the bathroom is right there, remember?"

"Right," she said, letting him believe she only needed to pee. 'I forgot." She hoped he would fall back asleep so she could gather her things and slip out while he slept. Looking over, she saw him watching her, propped up on an elbow, obviously aware that she wasn't looking for the bathroom.

"Hey," he said, scooching his body across to her side of the bed and reaching out to lay a hand on her arm. "Come here." Despite herself, Sage sat back down and let Rowan pull her back down to lie on the pillow. "What's going on?" He stroked the hair away from her face and placed a gentle kiss on her cheek, calming her heart and slowing her breathing.

"Rowan, I can't stay here all night. I never should have let you convince me to stay." It wasn't his fault. She was an adult and made her own choices, but he had been more than convincing with those magical hands while he helped her wash in the shower.

"I don't understand. Why not?"

She huffed, irritated that she had to explain it out loud, when in her head it all just made sense. "Your five-year-old daughter is sleeping just down the hall from here."

He kissed her cheek again, then her temple, sliding one hand under the covers and placing it on her stomach. "It's three o'clock in the morning. She'll be asleep for at least another three hours. Maybe four, as tired as she was from yesterday. But even if she was awake right this second, I would still want you to stay here with me." He kissed her jaw and slid his hand under her shirt, gently fondling her breast.

She would never make it out of his house if he continued to touch her like that. Hell, she'd never make it out of his bed with the way he touched her. "What about your mother?"

"What about her?"

"This is her house. What's she going to think of me spending the night here?"

Rowan was entirely awake, and he sat up in bed, not bothering to cover his body. "Well, after she comes home from sleeping at her boyfriend's house, she probably won't say anything except, 'I could really use a shower and a cup of coffee.' And, since we're not teenagers, I'm guessing she won't care one way or another if you're here." The bed moved slightly when Rowan ran his hand through his hair then let it fall to the bed. "Now, if you're done telling me a bunch of bullshit excuses, do you want to tell me the real reason you're running away from me?"

Why couldn't any of this be easy? Why couldn't she just lean into whatever was happening and be happy? Why couldn't she open up and be completely honest with him?

Why was she so afraid?

"I'm not running away," she said, pulling the sheets tighter across her chest.

He huffed out a soft laugh. "You were trying to sneak out of my house in the middle of the night. Wearing my clothes. Sorry if that looked a little like running away to me."

"We were supposed to be keeping things casual," she said. "Sleeping naked next to you in your bed doesn't feel completely casual to me." Her voice had taken on a hard edge. It was the only way she could keep it from shaking when she spoke.

"You keep asking me why I moved here," she said. "I moved here because I needed to get away from all the shitty guys I kept finding myself with." She sucked in a deep breath and let it go. "Joe? He was a gaslighter and a total dick. Tyler? Well, Tyler was a controlling and manipulative asshole. And let's not forget Drew, who only showed up to have sex when his schedule allowed it because..." The tears fell, her voice trembled, and she didn't care since the dam had broken and it was all coming out. "Because he was fucking married." Throwing her hands in the air, the blanket fell but she quickly pulled it back. "That's why I moved here, Rowan. To get away from that... that... toxicity that was eating me alive. I needed to get away from there and spend time on myself, my art, my business, my life.

"But then you came along and, once you stopped being a complete asshole to me, charmed my pants right off. Literally." She pulled in a stuttering breath and wiped her nose on the hem of her shirt. "And I let it happen. I let you do it. More to the point, I loved when you did it," she said, her voice barely above a whisper. "And truthfully, it's killing me being so close to you right now."

She wanted him to do something, say something. Hold her, hug her. Hell, he could have thrown her out the door and tossed her clothes out the window onto the front lawn and it would have been something.

"Why do you even like me?" she said, her frustration boiling over. "Why didn't you just keep being mean and let me go on about my life?"

Rowan

"You want to know what I like about you?" he said, turning his body to face her in the dark room.

"Yes!"

"That's easy," he said. "You've never given me shit about living in my mother's house. If I recall correctly, I don't think you've ever even asked me why I live here at my age." He'd never offered up the information to her and she never asked.

"I figured it wasn't really my business, but that it was most likely a childcare thing," she said.

He wanted to push her onto her back and make love to her right then and there, and not stop until the sun came up, but that would have to wait. "When my ex-wife left, she also took her paycheck with her. I do all right for myself, but I couldn't swing the house payment, the utilities, the groceries, childcare, and every other fucking thing that a baby needs and still work full time. So, we sold the house and barely broke even with it, leaving me and Maisie to find some place I could afford along with all the rest of it."

Talking about money problems to someone as obviously well-off as Sage appeared to be, was a serious blow to his ego. "My mom stepped up and offered to let us move in here and she volunteered to help me take care of Maisie until we could find something else."

Everybody in his circle already knew his story but telling it to someone for the first time in years made some of those old wounds hurt all over again. The anger at Jessica for packing up and walking out of their daughter's life without looking back was still unforgivable in his eyes, but that was a battle for a different day.

Expecting to see pity in Sage's eyes, he was shocked to see pain instead. She was hurting for him and for Maisie.

She was an amazing woman with a generous and kind heart.

But there was still the money issue that made things between them more uncomfortable than they should. At least from his perspective.

"Like I said, I do all right for myself, and we'll find a place, but there's something I need to ask you." Chancing a glance at her, she stared straight ahead but nodded. He sucked in a deep breath, hoping to get the question out without being an obtrusive asshole about it. "You don't have to answer me if you don't want to."

"Just ask," she said.

"Watching you redo your house, paying me to do the electrical work, which feels weird now that we're sleeping together, by the way."

Sage laughed and it did his heart good to hear it.

"I'd have to work six months non-stop to afford that and all the furniture and bedding and dishes and kitchen shit you and Maisie bought."

"What are you asking me?"

"Is there really that much money to be made in photography?" he spit out, then grimaced at the tactlessness with which the question landed.

After being quiet for an eternity, she finally said, "I do pretty well for myself with my business. But, the money I used to buy the house and to buy all the furniture to put in it? That's all from my inheritance."

He'd never given any thought to Sage's life before she moved in across the street. She'd never mentioned her parents having passed and he wondered where the money came from.

"My grandparents had a lot of money. Like, a lot of money. So, between my dad, my aunt and the three grandkids, we all got kind of a lot of money when they passed away."

Resentment flared again in his belly at how easily she spoke of inheriting that kind of money—the kind of money that would allow her to buy a house, redo the whole thing, and fully furnish it without a moment's hesitation. Then he remembered the pain of losing his father and realized her money may have come with a boatload of pain. Reaching over, he rested his hand on her thigh. "I'm sorry," he said. "Was it recent?"

"Four years ago," she said. "My grampa died about five years ago, and without him my gram just sort of stopped living. She ended up sort of wasting away." Her exhale was the sound of sorrow. "Like she died of a broken heart, more than anything else."

"Shit. I really am sorry. That's fucking sad." Memories of his father's unexpected death haunted him, even six years later, and he was suddenly grateful that his mother had the support she did to keep on living after he died.

"It *was* fucking sad," she agreed. "My gramps was awesome, but my gram was just the best human ever." Her smile was sad, and it kicked Rowan in the heart. "She had the best sense of humor. She was whip-smart and really funny. I think she would have gotten along really well with your mom." Then she smiled a happy smile, and it kicked him in the heart all over again.

After pulling the covers down, he peeled the tee shirt off her and tossed it to the other side of the room, then lowered his mouth to her breasts again. He sucked her nipple into his mouth, swirled his tongue around until it hardened then released it, repeating his motions on her other breast.

"You are amazing," he said, nudging her shoulder so she would be on her back again allowing him to trail kisses down her belly. "You are kind." He kissed her directly above her belly button. "You are generous," he said, kissing just above her pubic bone. Hooking his fingers into the waistband of her sweats, he pulled them off and tossed them over his head somewhere.

Then he stretched one leg over her and straddled her, letting his erection press into her belly. "All that shit with those other guys? It's all history. They're gone. They don't exist anymore." With a practiced ease, he tilted his hips and angled into her with a gentle, but firm push.

Long, graceful fingers swept over his back, heightening the tingling sensations as his whole body reacted to her touch. Her breath was warm over the shell of his ear, her belly pressed into his own. Her lips sought out his cheeks, his chin, his lips over and over again, moaning into him as he devoured her mouth and her body at the same time.

Time ticked away as they lost themselves in each other, their own wounds making them all the more vulnerable and open to the pleasure they chased as a balm to soothe those hurts.

Eventually, as the sun began to brighten the eastern horizon, they slept.

Sage

S age blinked her eyes open to see she was alone in Rowan's big bed, still naked, and in desperate need of a shower. Without any clean clothes to put on afterward, she grabbed her bra from the random assortment of clothing that had been strewn around his room and headed into the bathroom. Folded in a neat pile on the countertop was a fresh bath towel, a pair of his sweatpants, a clean tee shirt, and a pair of his socks.

By the time she made it out to the hallway, the smell of fresh coffee lured her down the stairs. Maisie sat at the kitchen table, her feet swinging beneath the chair as she tried to shovel mouthfuls of cereal into her face. "But the commercial is almost over," she begged as she used her free hand to keep the cereal from falling out.

"Eat your breakfast," Rowan said. "You can go back in the living room when you're all the way done." He looked up from his seat across from Maisie then stood with a grin to greet Sage with a hug and a kiss on the cheek, letting his hand drift across her backside as he released her. "Coffee?" he asked, and she nodded.

"Sage!" Maisie moved as if she was going to jump from her chair until Rowan gave her a look that halted her mid-jump and brought a frown to her face. She grunted, plunked an elbow on the table, and spooned another bite of cereal into her mouth.

After giving Maisie a quick squeeze around the shoulders, Sage took a seat at the table. Rowan turned his back while he poured Sage's coffee and Maisie stuck her tongue out at him. Chuckling, Sage hid her mouth behind her hand as Rowan handed her a steaming mug of morning fuel.

"What's funny?" he asked.

Maisie stopped chewing and stared at Sage, pleading wordlessly not to rat her out. Sage peeked over at the television, then met Rowan's expectant eyes. "Just something silly on TV." She accepted the mug from him gratefully and threw a quick smile in Maisie's direction before she stood to grab the milk from the fridge.

Maisie giggled. "You look funny."

Sage peered down at her baggy outfit and smiled. "What do you mean? I make this look good," she teased.

Maisie rolled her eyes and giggled again. "But those are my daddy's clothes. Why are you wearing Daddy's clothes?" Then she whispered loudly, "Those are boy clothes!"

Honesty was probably the best policy in this situation. Running her hand through her wet hair, she said, "I took a shower and wasn't thinking that I didn't have any of my own clean clothes to change into, so I had to borrow some of your dad's."

Maisie seemed satisfied with that answer and Sage returned to the table to finish drinking her coffee. Maisie tilted her head, her brows drawn together, and said, "Wait, did you have a sleepover here?" She turned to Rowan, her face scrunched in anger. "Daddy, that's not fair. You said I can't have any sleepovers. Why can you have them, and

I can't?" Fire burned in Maisie's eyes, but Sage was relieved that it burned toward Rowan and not her.

"Sorry, baby girl. I'm the dad and I make the rules." He reached over and plucked Maisie's bowl from the table. "You finally done here, or what?" he said, tipping the bowl to see how much she'd eaten. "Looks like you did a pretty good job on the Cheerios. You can go watch your show for a little while."

"Yes!" Maisie yelled and scrambled down from her chair. She raced into the living room, plopped onto a light blue fuzzy beanbag chair in the middle of the floor. She was adorable in her daisy-print night-gown, with her long blond hair sticking out in every direction as she settled into her chair and giggled every few seconds at whatever show she watched. Thankfully, she seemed to have forgotten all about the sleepover question.

While Sage watched Maisie, she felt Rowan's eyes on her. Placing his hand on top of hers, he said quietly, "How'd you sleep?"

Memories of the night before warmed her body better than any cup of coffee ever could. "Fine, thanks," she said, focused on watching the cartoon dog on the screen in front of Maisie. "You?" she asked, finally facing him, calmed by the warmth in his eyes.

"Like I haven't in a long, long time." He grinned, grabbed her coffee, and took a sip. "Yikes, no sugar?" She shook her head, and he handed the mug back to her. After washing down her coffee with a sip of his own, he said, "Got any plans for next weekend?"

With a shrug, she said, "I don't know yet. I've got a few things I need to do this week on the house, so it depends what's left by Saturday. Why?"

"Remember?" Maisie yelled from the living room. "It's my birth-day party. Daddy said I could invite you!"

Rowan smiled. "I don't want to take you away from your work but if you're around and you want to come hang out, Maisie and I would like it if you could be here. Pretty sure my mother would too."

"I don't want to intrude on your party," she whispered. "I wouldn't even know anyone there."

"You'd know us," he said, leaning over to kiss her cheek, taking an extra few seconds to nuzzle the sensitive spot beneath her ear. "But if you'd rather move furniture at home, that's cool."

From her beanbag chair, Maisie yelled, "Please can you come, Sage? Then you can see my friends."

It seemed she had no choice but to be at Maisie's party on Saturday and all the work on her house and her photography would have to be done by Friday night. She still hadn't told Rowan about the potential show at Millie's gallery, for no other reason than she was scared to bring it up. Going back to Boston had been on her mind quite a bit lately but with everything happening with Rowan, her heart was conflicted about what she wanted more. Her inability to pick well when it came to men only added to her confusion.

Rowan

Since his and Sage's heart-to-heart in the middle of the night, Jess had been on his mind. Not that he missed her, because he absolutely did not. It was more a sense of wondering how a person could pack up and leave their life behind. She called occasionally, but always during school hours when Maisie wouldn't be around. They never talked for long, and Rowan always ended the conversation feeling like shit. It was a tough way to have a relationship with someone, if you could call it a relationship. It was more like an acquaintanceship that he wished he didn't have to have anymore.

Thursday afternoon, in the middle of his workday, when Maisie would be nowhere around, his phone rang. Thinking it was his mother, or maybe Sage, though she usually texted, he stopped what he was doing to answer it.

"Hey, Rowan," Jessica said. "How's it going?"

Fuck. "What's up, Jess? I'm working right now, and Maisie isn't with me."

"Sorry to bother you while you're working." If she was sorry, it would be the first time in her life she was sorry about anything. She hesitated a few seconds before she said, "I just wanted to let you know I'm getting married again."

"Congratulations," he said, his voice flat. "Anything else?"

There was silence on the other end of the line. "No," she said. "I guess not. I just figured you'd want to know."

"Well, now I know." He didn't need to know, and he didn't care what she did.

"Right... OK... Bye."

His track record of feeling like shit after he spoke with Jess stayed a perfect one hundred percent. The difference between this time and all the other times, though, was Sage. Normally after he talked to Jess, he walked around in a pissed off mood for a couple of days and wouldn't talk to anyone about it, not even Marcus.

"Hey, man, I've got to head out of here. I'll be back tomorrow first thing."

"Everything all right?" Marcus asked as he finished hooking up one of the huge industrial stoves in the Faraway Inn's new kitchen.

"I'm good," he said. "I'll see you tomorrow."

Less than half an hour later, Rowan was climbing the steps to Sage's front door. He needed to see her, to touch her, just hold her in his arms. And maybe do a little kissing.

Like she often did, she had the screen door closed but the main door open to let in the warm air. Just before he knocked, Sage's voice caught his ear. She was on the phone with someone.

"This is going to be fantastic," she said. "I went up to the falls a couple weeks ago and I was able to get some really incredible shots."

She was silent as the person on the other end spoke.

"I can definitely do that. If I send them out to be framed from here, I can pick them up when I get back to town."

Silence again.

"No, I still have my apartment in Brookline." A slight pause. "Why would I get rid of it? Where else am I going to go?" Another pause. "I still haven't all the way decided. There's a lot to consider, you know?"

Rowan's hand hung in the air, frozen and unable to move. Was she leaving? Now? And if not now, was she leaving the door open to going back to Boston? Clearly, she didn't see Hazelton as home, and that hit Rowan like a blow to the gut.

"Rowan," she called from the kitchen. Then to the person on the phone, "Hey, Millie, can I call you back a little later?"

Pulling the door open, he stepped inside, his body moving of its own accord because his mind was still reeling from what he'd just heard.

"What are you doing here in the middle of the day?" Her eyes focused on his and her brows furrowed. "What's the matter? Is everything OK?"

Reaching out to hug him, she stopped when he said, "Who were you talking to just now?"

"What? Why?"

"It sounded an awful lot like you were talking about going back to Boston."

A look of surprise flashed across her features before it was immediately replaced by anger. "Were you listening to my private conversation?"

"Your door was open."

Her lips pressed into a line. "Yes, but most people would make themselves known rather than eavesdrop on someone else's conversation. What the hell, Rowan?"

"You still didn't tell me who you were talking to." She wasn't the only one who could be pissed off in the situation. Anger burned his stomach waiting to see if she would answer him.

"And there's no reason I have to," she said. "That was a personal conversation—"

"Yeah, you said that already," he cut in.

Her head snapped up and she pulled her shoulders back. In a voice that was too controlled and way too calm, she said, "I think maybe you ought to go and come back another time when you're not feeling like a jealous dick."

Jealous? He wasn't jealous. He was fucking angry. "How am I the one in the wrong here?" he snapped, heat coursing through his body, bringing a line of sweat to the hairline at the back of his neck. "You're the one keeping shit from me."

"Keeping shit?" she yelled. "Listen, I don't owe you anything. I am a grown woman with a life of my own, thank you very much. Who I speak with on the phone is not your business. When and why I go back to my own apartment is also not your business."

The phone call from Jess had him rattled and he was taking it out on someone who didn't deserve it. Again. He shoved a hand through his hair to brush away the pieces that had fallen in his face while he stared at the floor. "Fuck," he said. "You're right. You're right and I'm sorry."

"Thank you," she said, and tentatively took a step closer. "Are you all right? You look really frazzled. Is it really just because you overheard a phone call?"

Sage wasn't Jess and it wouldn't be fair to compare them. Pushing down his discomfort, he reached out to pull Sage into his arms. Just the feeling of her body against his helped to calm his racing heart. A quick sniff of her hair and everything was OK again. Mostly.

"It's been a weird day," he said, holding onto her a little tighter. "Sorry I dropped by without telling you I was coming over."

Leaning back so she could look up at him, the expression on her face was one of concern. "You don't have to tell me you're coming over. I like surprises." She stood on tiptoe and kissed his cheek. "I just don't like people listening to my private conversations and then questioning me about them."

"I get it," he said. Looking around the room, he noticed that she had started the renovations on the first floor. "Hey, you got the walls all patched up. Does that mean you're going to start painting soon?"

Her head waffled back and forth. "That was the original plan," she said, finally disengaging from his hold. "But, obviously you heard my phone call earlier, so now you know I'm planning to head back home so I can get my stuff together for the next show."

"How long are you going to be gone for?" His tone was clipped but he didn't know how to stop it.

"I don't know. I haven't thought that far out. I just have so much work to do and all my good equipment is back home."

What was even happening? They'd gotten so close and, he thought, they'd been moving in a positive direction together.

"Maybe a few weeks. Maybe more. I just don't know."

"Right," he said, and it sounded anything but right. Talking wasn't what he needed. Movement. Something physical to work out some of his shitty mood. Looking around the living room, he asked, "Need any help pulling up the old rug?"

Working mostly in silence, he ripped the carpet off the tack strips along the walls and she cut it into strips then rolled them up, stacking them on the porch to be put into the dumpster.

After tossing the last few carpet pieces into the dumpster, he stomped back up the porch steps. The exertion of work had helped but he still couldn't stop the grating irritation his day had caused.

"What do you think?" he asked, walking through the door. "Want to get the hallway and your bedroom carpets while we're already dirty?"

"Sure, unless you want to get really dirty," she said, doing her best hip swing as she neared him.

It was the worst thing she could have asked from him. There wasn't a time when he didn't want to tear her clothes off and watch her lose herself with him, but he couldn't do it. Not while his temper simmered the way it did. "No, not really," he said, stepping around her to start working in the hallway.

Her whole body shrunk before his eyes as she took a step back. Schooling her face to hide the shock and, most likely, humiliation, she said, "You know what, why don't we skip the rugs for today. I have a lot of work I need to get done, if it's all the same to you." Folding her arms over her chest she stood at the entrance of the hallway and waited for him to leave.

"It won't take long to get this done and I know the dumpster guy is coming back in the next few days." He squatted down to pull at the edge of the rug.

"Really," she said. "You can stop now." He kept going. "Rowan. Stop."

Standing and brushing past her, he said, "Whatever. Do it yourself, then."

As he pushed open the door, she called out to him. "Why did you come here?" He stopped on the porch but didn't turn around. "This afternoon, when you should have been working, you came here instead. Why?"

His shoulders slumped, then he straightened them again. If he could have started this day over, he'd have done it in a second and done it all differently. "I just wanted to see you."

Sage

Over the course of the week since Rowan's weirdness, Sage managed to get rid of the rest of the carpeting, as well as have the new appliances delivered and installed. The first coat of paint was drying and her motivation to do more was waning. The sun was high and bright; a beautiful day lay just outside her door.

Grabbing her camera and phone, she took off to find something else to photograph. She'd found a nature preserve online and going there would give her something to focus on other than her half-painted bedroom and whatever was happening with Rowan.

Driving along big, empty, wide roads with endless green on every side was as different from driving in Boston as day was to night. Again, feeling nostalgic about her apartment and her life back in the city, she called Julia and talked through the speakers as she drove.

"Sage, my home renovation friend, how is life treating you in the weeks since I've been there?"

Hearing Julia's voice calmed her racing thoughts. "I'm good, Jules," she said. "But I miss you. When are you coming out for another visit?"

After a few seconds of quiet, Julia said, "Looking at my calendar, I'm not sure it's going to be anytime soon. I've got open houses scheduled for the next few weeks and my client load is picking up." She sighed. "Work is stupid."

Sage laughed. "It is, but it's what we do, right?"

"Oh? Are you working again?"

"I'm on my way to get some shots at a local nature preserve because I've got a show coming up at the end of the month. I don't think my regular customers are going to be interested in my renovation pics."

"Good for you," Julia said. "It's good to hear you sounding more like your old self again. See, maybe moving out there for a few months was the right choice. Any idea when you're coming back home?"

Sage turned off the main road to follow the GPS toward the parking lot of Oxbow Preserve. With a sigh, she said, "I haven't decided yet."

"You are coming home, though, right?"

"Yeah," she replied. "I think."

"OK, girly, tell me what you're not telling me," Julia said. "I've got fifteen minutes until I have to meet my client, so spill it."

If there was one person on earth who could understand when Sage was not saying something, it would be Julia. "Remember that guy with the little girl?"

Julia huffed out a laugh. "Oh, I remember him alright, Mr. Epic Penis. Wait," she said, the pitch of her voice rising. "Is this about him?"

"Kind of."

A hushed screech came through the speakers as Julia tried to keep her excitement contained. "I knew it, I knew it, I knew it," she said. "How could you spend time around that guy and not get with him." She was quiet for a second and added, "Oh, Sage, have you gone and fallen in love with this guy?"

"No," she yelled. "Definitely haven't fallen in love. But we did kiss, and we've had sex."

"Just once?" Julia asked.

"Oh, no," Sage admitted. "We kinda have sex all the time."

Pulling her car into the gravel parking lot, shrouded by tall trees, she waited for Julia to respond to her confession.

"OK," Julia said slowly. "So, you had sex with him, and you aren't in love with him, yet he's the reason you aren't moving back home, even though you think you want to come home? I'm a little lost here, babe."

"That makes two of us, babe."

"Oh, I get it," Julia said. "It's complicated, isn't it?"

Sage wrapped her hands around the steering wheel, rested her head against the top of it. "Yes." Sitting upright again, she sighed and said, "When it started, I told him I wasn't looking for a relationship, that we had to keep it completely casual."

"But you've changed your mind?"

"Not really. But kind of. It kind of just got more serious than I anticipated." She dropped her head to the steering wheel again, her brain tired from trying to figure everything out. "I never wanted another relationship out here."

"I got you," Julia said. "So, you're looking for someone to hang out with, have a good time with, have sex with... you know, the usual."

"Yeah."

"So... a relationship?" Julia said.

Sage's brain hurt. "I don't know what I want. When I first met him, he was such an asshole, I just wanted him to go away and leave me alone. Now that I know him better, I don't know. I kinda like hanging around with him. And the sex was frickin' incredible."

Julia's laughter filled Sage's little car. "His penis was epic, wasn't it?"

"Oh my God, Jules, you have no idea!" The friends laughed together like they always did, and Sage missed being near her. "Jules, what do I do? My gut instinct with guys is total shit. They all seem great and shiny at the beginning and then... they turn out to be entitled jerks or controlling assholes, or...married! I don't know if I'm up for another relationship attempt, Jules." She breathed out sigh from the bottom of her soul, Rowan's pissy attitude from the other day front and center in her mind.

She couldn't shake the feeling that there was still something he wasn't telling her.

"Alright, bestie, I have about two minutes until I need to go but I got you covered. This is what you should do. Just relax. You said you were friendly with his family, so hang out with them too. Pay attention to the people around him and you'll see what kind of guy he really is. Then you'll be able to make an informed decision."

"His little girl invited me to her birthday party tomorrow. Think I should go?"

"Yes! One hundred percent you should go."

Sage drew in a deep breath, sighed it out. "I miss you. You and Ty totally need to come out for a visit when you finally have a free weekend."

Most of Sage's evening was spent editing and retouching the photos she took at the preserve. Several of them held a ton of potential for the upcoming show. The more she worked, the more excited she became to get back to Boston and the more conflicted her heart became.

Rowan

"I think you're out of your mind, dude," Marcus said as he and Rowan leaned against the edge of the picnic table.

The house had been decorated like a childhood dream. Balloons had been tied to the porch spindles, the light post at the end of the driveway, the mailbox, and the backs of all the chairs that had been set up around several round tables in the driveway. Brightly colored tablecloths covered the tables, streamers ran along the front of the garage, and several large coolers had been set up next to a long buffet table loaded with stacks of plates, napkins, forks and knives, and several bowls of chips and other snacks.

The main attraction, however, was an enormous blow-up bounce house that had been erected on the sprawling front lawn.

As more guests arrived, Maisie, Finn, and Sage were throwing beanbags at corn hole boards, not having much luck with scoring, but laughing hysterically as they tried.

Rowan couldn't tear his eyes away from them. "I don't think I am." He jutted his chin in the girls' direction. "I mean, look at them."

"Yeah, I see them. They're crazy about each other. Which is why I think you're fucking crazy to even think about ending things with her. Granted, I don't know her all that well, but what I've seen of her with the kid, not to mention how different you are since you're together, I'm lost as to why you'd want to end that."

He hadn't been able to tell his mother, so telling Marcus would be the first time he'd said the bitter-tasting words out loud. "She's going back to Boston."

"For what?" Marcus asked. "Like, she's selling the place and leaving? Or she's going back for a visit and then coming back?"

"I don't know."

Marcus smacked him on the arm. "Then why the fuck don't you ask her? 'Cuz I don't think that's an off-limits question to ask the woman you're in love with."

"I'm not in love with her," Rowan spat out and those words tasted worse than the other ones.

"Ah," Marcus said. "Just using her for sex then?" He angled his head to leer at Sage. "I can certainly see why."

Rowan's vision burned red as he spun, grabbed Marcus's shirt, then froze at the stupid smile on his friend's face. Immediately Rowan released his grip on Marcus's shirt and returned to his place next to him.

"Oh yeah," Marcus said with a laugh, straightening the wrinkles out of his shirt. "You're definitely not in love with her."

"Fuck off," Rowan spat out, then down a mouthful of beer.

So what if he was in love with Sage? He'd been in love before and look where that got him: a single parent living in his mother's house, working to scrape together enough savings to buy a house. A thought crossed his mind, and the guilt of the thought almost kept him from saying it aloud. "Maybe if she leaves, I'll finally get the house, huh?"

"Is that really what you want?" Marcus asked, stuffing a jalapeno popper into his mouth. "The house and not the girl to go with it?"

Recently arrived, Erica Becker and Amy Navarro walked by the table, following behind their children. "Hey, Rowan," Erica purred as she sidled up beside him. "Beautiful day, isn't it?" Her red fingernails looked like drops of blood when she laid her hand across his forearm. Leaning over Rowan, she said, "Hi, Marcus, nice to see you again," then stood tight against Rowan's side.

Marcus nodded. With raised eyebrows, in an almost-whisper, he said to Rowan, "Seriously?"

Rowan peeled Erica's hand off his arm. "I need something inside. Anyone else need anything?"

Amy, Marcus, and Erica declined his offer, though Erica did so with an exaggerated pout that turned Rowan's stomach. Walking over to Sage and the kids, he stopped and rested his hand on Sage's back. The tug of war in his heart raged even as she leaned back into his hand. "How's my birthday girl doing?"

"We're good, Daddy. Right, Sage?" Maisie said.

"We're good," Finn parroted.

"Right," Sage agreed, but with noticeably less enthusiasm than Maisie had. Her expression was guarded as she turned to him. "How's your day going?" With one simple question she had called him on his bullshit yet again, this time letting him know she noticed that he'd been ignoring her since she arrived. It wasn't his plan; it was simply how his moody brain worked.

"It's good." Turning toward the house, he said, "I'm grabbing a soda. Can I get you anything?"

"No thanks. Maisie, Finn, and I have a game to finish."

He was the one contemplating breaking up with her, so why did it piss him off so much that she effectively dismissed him?

Sage

Rowan had come back outside and stood beside Marcus at the grill, but Sage had had enough of his toddler temper tantrum. If she'd wanted to be ignored, she could have stayed home and gotten her bedroom painted and probably the whole hallway too. She came to this party because he'd invited her, and she'd hoped they'd be able to talk things through a little bit. Evidently, that wasn't Rowan's plan.

"Sweetheart, I have to go to the ladies' room. Why don't you and Finn go play with your other party guests."

Rather than wait in line to use the bathroom on the main floor, Sage went up to use the one in Rowan's room. As she came back down the stairs, two women were having a conversation from what sounded like the kitchen.

"God, he's delicious, isn't he?" one woman said. "I could literally eat him alive."

Sage chuckled to herself at the woman's open desire for some lucky guy.

"Too bad he's with that other woman though," the second woman said. "I haven't met her, but she seems nice enough."

The first woman snorted. "Nice? Who cares about nice?" Chuckling, she said, "I don't think he's really all that into her."

"What makes you say that? How can you even know that?"

"I've got eyes and I've got ears. I just heard him talking about it," the first woman said, and Sage's ears perked up at the unfolding drama. "You know she bought the house he was going to buy."

A rock landed in Sage's stomach at the comment, her balance suddenly unsteady as she gripped the handrail to keep her knees from buckling.

"So?" the friend said.

"So... guy wants house. Girl buys house. Guy fucks girl to get house."

The woman's singsong voice as she turned what happened between Sage and Rowan into some sort of fucking nursery rhyme brought a sudden wave of nausea to her stomach. Wrapping her arms around her waist, Sage folded over and sat, trying to take enough oxygen into her lungs.

She had no idea he'd wanted that house.

That explained everything, starting from his horrible attitude at the diner.

"You really think that's what happened?" the friend whisper-shouted.

"Obviously," the first woman said. "I've been after him for how long? And he's never been interested. Suddenly this woman shows up and buys the house he wants and the next thing they're a couple? Please! He's clearly only fucking her to get the house." She chuckled again. As their footsteps crossed the wood floor, their voices got quieter. "I even heard him tell Marcus that he might actually have a shot at the house, now, because she's leaving." The side door to the kitchen opened and closed, leaving Sage alone in stunned silence as tears burned their way down her cheeks.

In a haze, she made her way down the stairs, through the kitchen, and out to the front yard. On unsteady feet, she concentrated on taking one step at a time to get past the bounce house, across the yard, through the line of cars, and out to the street.

"Everything all right?"

Not knowing if the voice was talking to her, she looked up to see Marcus walking toward her from a little further down the road. His eyes were fixed on hers, trying to get a read on the situation.

"Me? Oh yeah," she said. "Fine."

Marcus stopped in front of her. "You sure? No offense, but you don't look fine."

"What every woman wants to hear," she joked.

He smiled but the way his brow furrowed, it was more a smile of concern, not humor. "Did he do something or say something stupid?" He shook his head slowly, perhaps knowing Rowan's intentions all along. "We've been friends a long time but I'm not above kicking his ass if I have to."

Marcus seemed to be a nice guy, but she still wasn't interested in dragging him into whatever was happening between her and Rowan. Although, after the information she picked a few minutes ago, it was clear there wasn't anything happening between her and Rowan. Not anymore.

"Thanks, Marcus," she said. "I appreciate your offer and maybe I'll keep it in my back pocket in case I need it later." Tears threatened to slip from her eyes, so she took a few steps past him, desperate to get back to the safety of her own home.

"Does Rowan know you're out here?"

Like it made any difference what Rowan did or didn't know. She shrugged. "Don't know. Don't care."

She didn't need to pack much; she was in her Prius and on the road within thirty minutes of getting home, her hands-free call to Julia the first thing she did once she hit the highway. "I think it's time to put the house back on the market, Jules," she said through more tears. "Things just didn't work out."

Rowan

For the third time that afternoon, and what felt like the millionth time in the past two weeks, Maisie was crying. He didn't mean to keep snapping at her, or anyone else, but it didn't stop him from doing it. "I'm sorry, Zee," he said, reaching out to pull her in for a hug.

As tears streaked down her face, she wrapped her arms around her middle and pulled away from him. "No," she said. "You're being mean. I don't like you." As Rowan's busted heart took another hammer strike, Maisie ran into his sister's arms instead of his.

"Jesus, Rowan," Erin said, holding his crying daughter. "What the hell is the matter with you?"

Maisie had slept at Erin's place the night before under the pretense of helping to babysit Finn. Delores had planned to spend the night at Adam's house and Rowan saw the opportunity to take advantage of a night to himself. Not that it did much good. All he did was stew over the fucking mess he'd made of things with Sage as well as feel like shit for being such a bear to everyone he knew since she left.

But what he couldn't figure out, and she never answered his texts or calls to explain, was why she felt the need to leave for Boston in the middle of a party without even saying goodbye.

Marcus had told him she'd gone but by the time the party ended, and he'd made it to her place, her car was gone, and the doors were locked up tight.

"Nothing's the matter," he yelled at his sister. "I'm fucking fine."

Maisie howled and Erin's eyes blazed. "Come on sweet girl," she said into Maisie's ear, though her eyes were fixed on his and promised murder if he opened his mouth to speak. "Let's get out of here for a little while. I think Daddy needs a timeout to get himself together."

She carried Maisie to the door, looked over her shoulder. "Finny should stay asleep while we're gone. But if he wakes up, please don't yell at him and make him cry or we're going to have serious words, Rowan Kennedy," Erin said, anger threading through her words, as she carried Maisie out the door.

Finn had fallen asleep in the car and rather than leave him out there while she visited, Erin had carried him up to the travel crib Delores kept for him in Maisie's room.

Watching Erin walk away with Maisie shredded his heart again but stopping them would only cause more tears, so he let them be. "He'll be fine," Rowan said. "We'll be fine."

Rowan threw his feet on the coffee table and shot off another string of texts to Sage.

> Why did you leave in the middle of the party

> Hey can you at least tell me what I did wrong

> Are you planning to come back or are you staying in Boston

Her continued lack of response told him everything he needed to know. He'd fucked up. She told him about the string of shitty guys she'd been dating and then he went and turned into one of them himself. No fucking wonder she left. But what he still couldn't understand is why she left in the middle of Maisie's party, and she wasn't going to do him any favors by telling him.

She most likely was going to stay in Boston, though how he knew that he wasn't sure. Call it a gut feeling.

Fine. Fuck it. If that's how it was going to be then that was his new reality. Tossing his phone onto the table he grabbed the clicker and turned on the news, simply so he wasn't alone with his thoughts anymore.

At some point in the next hour, heavy footsteps in the kitchen drew his attention and he turned to see Marcus staring at him as he walked through the room.

"What are you doing here?" Rowan said, turning his attention back to the television.

"Your sister sent me a text. Said you were in need of an ass-kicking. Making small children cry and shit like that."

"She's my kid. She cries all the fucking time."

"Maybe, but it sounded like you were being more of an asshole than usual." Marcus sat on the couch next to Rowan's chair. "What the fuck happened with you two?"

"She was being a pain in the ass, and I yelled. Happens every day. Not as big a deal as my sister's making it out to be."

"Not the kid, you stupid ass," Marcus said. "You and Sage."

"What's the difference? She's gone and I'm here." He chucked his chin in the direction of his phone. "She won't answer a single fucking text and she won't pick up when I call. So, I have no idea what happened between us."

Marcus leaned forward, elbows on his knees. "You didn't say anything to her at the party? Because she was pretty upset when I saw her leaving."

He'd wracked his brain nonstop over the two weeks she'd been gone. The last thing he'd said to her was his offer to bring her a drink from the kitchen. "What, like how I wanted to end things with her?"

"Something like that," Marcus said.

Rowan shook his head. Though he'd been thinking about it, he couldn't bring himself to act on it. The thought of losing her hurt too fucking bad. "Nope. Nothing. I asked if she wanted a drink. She said no and that was the last thing we said to each other. It was the last time I saw her. I didn't even know she left until you told me."

Squeezing his forehead with his fingers, Rowan tried unsuccessfully to ease the headache that had taken up permanent residence there.

"Mama! Help! I waked up!" Finn's voice called out through the baby monitor.

"Want me to go get him?" Marcus asked.

Rowan pushed himself to standing. "That's alright, I've got him."

"Wonin, Wonin!" His nephew screeched and jumped up and down in the crib when Rowan walked in.

"Finn, buddy. How you doin'?" Rowan said as he scooped the little guy into his arms.

"I good," Finn said, nodding his head. He threw his arms around Rowan's neck, pecked his cheek with a kiss. Holding the chubby toddler offered a certain comfort. The unconditional love children shared could almost melt even a stone-cold heart like his own.

He felt like even more of a dick for making Maisie cry as he changed Finn into a dry diaper before he brought him downstairs to wait for Erin and Maisie to come back.

He owed everybody an apology—his mother, his sister, and most importantly, Maisie.

As Finn munched a cup of Cheerios watching television in Rowan's lap, Marcus asked, "What's next?"

"How do you mean?"

"With you and Sage. You going after her or what?"

The side door opened, and Maisie bolted through to Rowan's side, her face dirty with streaks of pink. "Daddy, Auntie bought me an ice cream. It was strawberry."

As if he hadn't behaved like a raging bull for the past two weeks, Maisie seemed to forgive him without him even asking. He didn't deserve a kid so sweet. But she deserved to be treated better than he'd been doing.

"That's awesome, Zee. Did you say thank you to Auntie?"

She nodded.

"That's my girl," he said, touching a hand to her soft but sticky cheek. "Hey, Zee, I'm sorry I've been really grouchy the last couple of weeks. I haven't been very nice to you or Grandma or anyone else and that's not OK. I've been a little bit sad and sometimes my sad comes out as mad."

Maisie's little arms wrapped around his neck, and she kissed his cheek. "That's OK," she said. "Sometimes my sad comes out as mad too."

He truly didn't deserve her.

"How is everything here?" Erin said, smiling at Finn stretched out in Rowan's lap, his hand in the Cheerio bowl.

Rowan brushed Finn's hair back, letting the delicate strands fall. "We're good, right buddy?"

"Yup," Finn said without taking his eyes off of Sesame Street.

Erin turned to Marcus, questioned him with a look. Marcus shrugged and she sat down next to him on the couch.

"So, what's your next play?" she said to Rowan.

"I don't have one," he said. "It's over and there's nothing I'm going to do about it."

"You don't think she's coming back?" Erin asked. She'd only met Sage a couple times, but somehow Sage managed to wrap her in that magic spell she seemed to cast over everyone she met. "What about the house?"

"Who's not coming back?" Maisie asked. "Miss Sage?"

Rowan looked at his daughter's pleading eyes but had no choice but to nod.

"Why not? Doesn't she like me anymore?"

Fuck. Mentally he made a note to stick to his 'no dating until Maisie is in college' rule. It wasn't fair for her to get hurt because he and Sage didn't work out.

Marcus pulled Maisie to sit in his lap. "Miss Sage didn't leave because of you. Trust me. She is crazy about you," he told her.

Maisie looked up at him, eyes wide. "How come she left then?"

"Because of me, baby girl," Rowan said. "Miss Sage was mad at me and that's why she left. Uncle Marcus is right. She would never leave because of you."

"Daddy," Maisie said. "You should say you're sorry to Miss Sage too and then she will come back and be my friend again."

Erin and Marcus chuckled but neither of them told her she was wrong. "I don't even know where she is. I don't know where she lives."

"What about the show she has coming up? Can you look up the gallery? Maybe ask the owner," Marcus offered.

"They'd never give out that kind of information," Erin said. "At least I hope they wouldn't."

Rowan nodded, thinking through his options. "I don't think they'd tell me much," he agreed. "But maybe I can look up her friend. I know she's a real estate agent and her first name is Julia. That should be enough to go on, right?"

After a quick Google search, Rowan found Julia, and fifteen minutes after sending a message through her contact page, his phone pinged a reply.

Sage

It had only been two weeks since she'd left Hazelton, but it felt more like two years. In some ways it felt more like a dream, and occasionally she wondered if any of it was real. The unending texts that Rowan kept sending was her biggest clue that she hadn't dreamed it and that she'd made the right decision going back to Boston.

At least a few times a day she looked at the unread messages he'd sent and thought about blocking him outright, but some little piece of her heart that missed him wouldn't let her do it. Instead, she looked at them, hoping his heart was breaking, and went back to work, pretending her heart was wholly unscathed.

When her apartment buzzer rang, Sage stopped in front of the hall mirror one more time. After not wearing full makeup for so long while she worked on her house in Hazelton, she hardly recognized the woman staring back at her. Perfect smoky eye with dark mascara, deep red lipstick, and a touch of bronze on her cheek bones topped off the sexy evening look she'd been trying for.

Buzzing her in, Sage waited for Julia to knock on the apartment door, flutters of nerves swirling around her belly. It had only been about three months since she'd done a show at Millie's gallery, though her belly roiled as if she'd never done it before.

"Look. At. You." Julia took Sage's hands in her own, twirled her around like they were on a dance floor. "How do you manage to always look so stunning? I'm starting to be a little jealous, you know." Julia laughed as she released Sage's hands. "Seriously, babe, you look like a million dollars. You are going to be sold out of everything you have out there tonight just because of how hot you are."

Laughing, Sage hugged her, being careful not to wipe any of her make up onto Julia. "You think?"

"Oh, trust me. I don't think; I know."

The swirl of panic in Sage's belly settled, but not by much. "Is it weird to say I wish Rowan was here for this?" The heaviness that had taken up a home on her chest and shoulders suddenly weighed on her. "It's stupid, isn't it? He didn't even really want me, just my house, and somehow, I can't stop thinking about him."

Julia smiled and it was full of nothing but compassion. No judgment, no anger, no disappointment. "It's not stupid at all." She hugged Sage gently. "I know you really liked him."

Sage blinked rapidly to keep the tears from starting. "Don't make me cry, Jules," she said, dotting her eye with one careful finger. "I'll never be able to get my makeup this perfect twice in one day."

The friends laughed and Julia said, "Have you given any more thought to what you want to do with the house?"

Sage's posture slumped. "No," she admitted. "I don't really want to sell it, but I don't think I can go back there. Not right now. Not while Rowan still lives across the street."

Leaning against the table and with that same look of compassion, Julia said, "I know you heard some awful things about him, but did you ever think maybe they weren't true? Maybe he really did have feelings for you that ran deeper than wanting to get into your house."

"You mean like wanting to get into my pants?" Sage joked.

Julia smiled and a small laugh passed her lips. "Do you think... just maybe... he might possibly have found his way into your heart?"

Grabbing her bag from the hook by the door, she turned to Julia. "I thought maybe he did, but I don't know that I can overlook the fact that he did it by trying to use me to get into the house he wanted." Sighing deeply, she said, "I just don't know that I can overlook that." Quietly, she added, "No matter where it may have ended up."

As they exited the building and walked toward Julia's car, Sage had made up her mind. Originally, she needed a clean break from Boston, but it was time for a clean break from Hazelton. "I think I'm ready to put the place back on the market. You can list it whenever you're ready."

Nodding, Julia opened Sage's door then walked to the other side as Sage adjusted her dress and clicked her seatbelt.

"You don't think I should sell it, do you?" Sage asked as Julia pulled the car away from the sidewalk, heading them toward the gallery.

Julia made a noncommittal noise. "It's your house. Do what you want with it."

Her friend's sudden coolness and lack of usual support hit Sage. "What aren't you telling me?" she said. "Did you already plan on using my place for vacation or something?"

"No," she said. "It has nothing to do with me."

"What then?"

Julia was quiet for a second then she huffed out a breath. "Look, it's not up to me what you do with the house. But since you've been back here, you've been miserable. I don't know if you miss the house, the town... or the boy."

"I absolutely do not miss him, Jules," she said. "He was using me to get to the house. And if he wants it, fine, I'll put it on the market and sell it to him. He doesn't want me or need me once he has that." Bile rose in her throat, and she swallowed it back down as she thought of the things she and Rowan had done in that house, the way they christened every room in the place. If all he wanted was the house, she hoped those memories would play in his mind every single time he brought another woman home.

"Do you really believe that? That all he wanted was the house?"

"Yes." No? Maybe? "Why? You think that woman was lying? She had no idea I was even in the house when she said all that. Why would she be lying? Isn't it more likely that he was playing me from the very beginning and me, being me, was just too blind to see it?" Despite her attempts to stop them, the tears started to fall. Her makeup would be destroyed by the time they made it to the gallery. "I hate that I went and started to like him."

Quietly, Julia said, "You fell in love with him, you mean?"

A sob tore through her, makeup be damned.

Wrapping her arms around her middle, Sage curled over and let it all out. All the hurt, all the betrayal, all the self-disgust. All the longing and loneliness she couldn't shake since she'd left Hazelton. "Yes," she finally admitted.

"Lucky for you, I keep a makeup bag in my back seat at all times," Julia joked as she helped Sage clean up the disaster that was her makeup. Sage held a cold, wet paper towel to her eyes to try and lessen some of the puffiness, while Julia blended some moisturizer with the foundation she was about to apply to Sage's red cheeks.

"Millie's probably wondering where I am," Sage said as Julia brushed the last coat of mascara on Sage's lashes. "After seeing how I looked when I got here, she probably thinks I got mugged or something."

"No, she doesn't," Julia said. "I gave her the 'I've got this' look when we walked by. She knows we're coming back in a few minutes." Julia screwed the mascara wand back into the tube. "There," she said, looking Sage over from forehead to chin, then scanned the rest of her. "Well, at least the dress is a killer."

Sage burst out laughing and it felt so much better than crying, yet the tears weren't buried all that deeply. "Come on," she said, handing Julia's makeup bag back. "Let's get out of here so I can go make some money and some new connections."

Extremely self-conscious about the redness in her cheeks and the puffiness under her eyes that no amount of makeup could help, Sage tried to engage with the clientele coming through the gallery. Millie had told her there were going to be several buyers from some local businesses on site, as well as a few smaller hotels looking for new art for recently renovated properties.

By the end of the night, Sage had sold several of her prints, some to private customers and a whole bunch to corporate clients. More importantly, she had made quite a few new connections and had two appointments set up to discuss the decorating needs of a couple hotels who were looking to showcase more of the natural beauty of the state as a whole, not just Boston proper.

"This one's interesting," a warm and familiar voice said as Sage began cleaning up her space. Her entire body froze, afraid that when she turned around the illusion would be shattered, and she would know the person who spoke was not Rowan.

Rowan

E very frame in Sage's section of the gallery held a print of either a building or a landscape or a close up on a flower or tree or insect, except one. One frame looked as if it had been hung with nothing but a light gray paper behind the glass.

It had only been a couple of weeks but seeing her in the flesh was like being able to breathe after being held underwater for too long. Her back was to him as she tidied up her area. He shoved his hands into his pockets to keep them from touching her before he knew if she would welcome it. Odds were not in his favor.

When he spoke, she froze in place, her hand hovering over a framed print of Horsetail Falls that had been set on a small table. Her sharp intake of breath could mean one of two things. She recognized his voice and wanted to end him on the spot, or she recognized his voice and was going to make him work for any scrap of attention he was hoping to get from her.

Her back straightened and she ran her hands over her thighs, as if brushing away lint or trying to smooth non-existent wrinkles in her dress. It was a slow move; one she was most likely using to give herself time. Time for what, he didn't know, but he hoped it would be good.

Dressed in dark jeans and a blue buttoned shirt with the sleeves rolled up, he looked around at the formal clothes everyone else was wearing and didn't bat an eye. He wasn't there to look good or make friends. His only goal was to get Sage to speak with him. If she told him to go away, he would, but it needed to come directly from her mouth, not inferred from ignored texts and unanswered phone calls.

"What's it called?" he said, pointing to the seemingly empty frame.

"Invisible Hand Prints," she whispered without turning around.

Looking closer at the photo he realized he was looking at a blank wall; a wall that was the same color as the inside of the closet where he and Sage had the hottest, virtually silent, sex he'd ever had. The same closet where he made her keep her hands flush against the wall. His belly dropped and his jeans were suddenly way too tight.

Taking two steps closer, he reached out a hand to touch the back of her arm. "Sage, please look at me," he said. "Please just talk to me." She didn't speak but she didn't remove her arm from his grasp, so he counted that as a tentative win.

Her voice was barely audible when she finally responded. "Rowan, what are you doing here? How did you even know where to find me?"

Slowly she turned toward him, and his heart skidded in his chest. He'd never seen her in a full face of makeup and a dress that showed so much skin. His pants felt like they would split at the zipper if he kept looking at her curves.

But it was her eyes that brought him up short. The depth of the pain he saw in them cut him to his core. "Baby, please tell me what happened and why you left." Cautiously he reached a hand to cradle her face, ran his thumb along her cheek. Settling his heart, she closed her eyes and leaned into his hand.

Dreamily, she opened her eyes. "I don't want to get into this here," she said. "Julia's coming to get me in about ten minutes. Maybe we can meet up tomorrow and talk over coffee or something?"

Fuck that. He had her in his sights and he wasn't giving up until they figured it out. "Julia's actually not coming to get you," he said. "I'm bringing you home."

Her brow furrowed.

"Unless you don't want me to. Then I'll be more than happy to get you an Uber. But not before we talk. About everything."

Her head tipped to one side. "Did you guys set this up behind my back?" she asked.

"Yes."

A look of shock registered at his quick confession.

"I looked her up online and sent her a message. We talked for about an hour the other day. For obvious reasons she wouldn't tell me where you live but she was willing to tell me about the show and let me take my best shot."

One side of her mouth lifted as she breathed out a small laugh. "Fine," she said. "You can drive me home."

The blood drained from his head, leaving him almost giddy at her response.

"And we can talk," she added.

Talk. Kiss. Get naked. Make love until the sun comes up. He was up for any and all of it.

Aside from giving him directions, it took them about twenty silent minutes to make it from the gallery back to her apartment, a first-floor unit in a brownstone. He understood why she loved it as much as she did, and he worried it would be too much to ask of her to leave it behind. From its rounded living room full of windows overlooking the street, to its beautifully maintained hardwood floors and historic wood trim everywhere, to the giant fireplace, Rowan wondered what he could ever offer that could compare with any of what he saw.

Kicking off her heels as she led him toward the kitchen, she said, "Can I get you anything to drink? I'm parched."

"Sure."

They sat across from each other over her tile-topped kitchen table and Rowan couldn't take the silence anymore. "Can we talk now?"

She nodded. "You start."

With a laugh, he said, "I was hoping to say the same thing to you." Leaning forward he took the liberty of holding her hand. "Why did you leave me?"

She sighed deeply after taking a sip of water. "I didn't leave you, Rowan. I left Hazelton. My life is here, and this is where I need to be."

It wasn't the truth, and he knew it. At least it wasn't the whole truth. Julia had told him what had happened, he just needed Sage to get it off her chest and then let him explain what a conniving bitch Erica Becker was. "Bullshit."

Pulling her hand out from under his, she said, "Excuse me? Who do you think you are telling me my reasons are bullshit?" She stood and padded across the kitchen to refill her glass. Leaving his glass on the table, he got up and followed her.

"I called bullshit because you left in the middle of a fucking birthday party, Sage. That's not something you do if everything else is fine and you're just moving away. That's something you do when there's a problem that you don't want to face."

Her back was toward him, and he was tired of her hiding from him. "Turn around, Sage. Turn around and tell me to my face what the fuck happened that day."

"I think you need to leave," she said, her voice wavering.

"Fuck that," he said. "Not until we have this out. Not until you tell me what you're so afraid of." His tone was harsher than he intended but he wasn't about to apologize; she'd have to deal with his attitude.

"Me?" she yelled, wheeling on him. "You think I'm the one to blame for this?" Rage flamed in her eyes, and he was there for it. He wanted it. He wanted her to finally say what she wouldn't say. "You think this is about me?"

He stepped closer to her, pushing her backward until she bumped into the counter and had to stop moving. Gripping the countertop on either side of her hips, he boxed her in. "Then tell me what it is about," he said, keeping his voice low, hoping to entice her to keep talking.

Her eyes fluttered closed but then popped open again. "No," she said. "You can't just come into my house and try to seduce me." Emotion simmered below the surface, and he knew they were finally getting somewhere. "Not again," she said. "Because you can't have this house. This one is mine." One lovely hand with hot-as-fuck red fingernails flew to cover her mouth, as if she said something wrong.

Rowan

Keeping her trapped against the counter, he leaned in and spoke gently into her ear. "Is that what you think I did, Sage? You think I seduced you so I could have your house?" The hair by her neck fluttered with each word he spoke, and a visible shiver shuddered through her body. Pressing his thighs against hers, he nibbled the soft spot beneath her ear. "Do you really believe I only want you because you bought the house I wanted to buy?"

She swallowed and her chest shook with a stuttering breath. "Yes," she whispered. "Didn't you?"

"No, Sage, I didn't." Moving one leg so it rested between hers, he leaned back to look her in the eyes. "When I fucked you," he said, rubbing his thigh into the warmth between her legs, "and when I made love to you, I did it because I wanted you, Sage. I don't give a flying fuck about the house." He placed a tender kiss on her lips. "I wanted you beneath me, and on top of me, and bent over in front of me." Grabbing hold of her hands he said, "But mostly I just wanted you with me. I wanted you around me, near me."

Her eyes were wet with unshed tears, and he knew she'd been doing a lot of crying over the past couple weeks. He wanted to be the reason she laughed again.

"But that lady said—"

"I don't care what the lady said. She's just jealous because I fell in love with you and not her. It's as simple as that." Her hands were still firmly gripped in his own so she couldn't use them to wipe away the tears that had started to fall.

"It wasn't about the house?" she said through the tears. Shaking her head, she scrunched her eyes closed. "Wait," she said. "Did you just say you're in love with me?"

"I don't give a shit about the house, Sage. I'll burn the fucking thing to the ground if it'll prove to you that I don't care about it." He leaned down and kissed the stream of tears on one cheek and then the other. "I love you. When I go to sleep at night, it's not to thoughts of your house." Starting at the corner of her mouth, he kissed her lips, then moved down to her chin. Tipping her head back she gave him access to her neck, which he claimed with more soft kisses. "And certainly, when I jerk off, it is not to thoughts of your house."

Her fingers threaded through his hair while he continued to kiss her neck and all along her collarbone. "If it's not my house you think about when you do that, what do you think about?"

A raging fire tore through him from head to foot. "If you don't want me to rip this dress to shreds, you should probably take it off before I answer that question."

A timid smile played at her lips as she pushed him away then turned so her back was to him. "I need help with the zipper."

With barely controlled aggression, Rowan's thick fingers worked the tiny zipper from the nape of her neck down to the bottom of her ass, pushing the dress off her shoulders into a heap on the floor.

His heart beat so hard it threatened to break through his ribs as he stared at her exquisite form, specifically those perfectly full ass cheeks with the line of dark blue fabric between them. He would definitely be buying her more thongs, that was a no-brainer.

"This," he said, grabbing two handfuls of her ass. "This is what I think about. This perfect fucking ass." Moving his body against hers, he slid his hands around her waist, letting one hand slide down between her legs. "And this sweet pussy."

She gasped when he slipped his finger between her lips. "I think about that a lot. How hot it is," he said, dipping his finger into her. "How wet it gets for me."

The tension in her body eased as she melted into him, his strong arms holding her tightly with no intention of ever letting her go.

"My bedroom is off the living room if you want to go there," she whispered.

"Don't worry, we'll get there." Her hips gyrated, pressing herself into his hand. "But not until you tell me what you're so afraid of."

Her hips stilled and she sucked in a breath. "What do you mean? I already told you."

"Tell me again."

Her back and shoulders stiffened. "I thought you only wanted me for my house," she said with a huff.

"Right," he said. "I got that part, but that was something you could have just asked me about and I could've cleared that up right away. What aren't you telling me, Sage?" Slowly, he eased his finger along her center.

Through a whimper, she said, "You're distracting me. I can't think while you're doing that."

He grinned; his cheek pressed against her hair. "I don't want you to think. I want you to tell me what you're afraid of," he said, purposefully increasing his tempo.

"Rowan," she whined.

His finger slid inside her. "Stop stalling, Sage."

Stuttering breaths caused her body to shiver against his chest. The hand that had been laying against her belly moved up, cupped one breast while the other continued to move within her. The flimsy lace cup of her bra made it easy to feel her immediate response when he rubbed her nipple with the pad of his thumb.

"You tried to keep things casual with me, Sage," he murmured into her ear. "But that didn't work. I have never felt less casual about anyone or anything in my entire fucking life and neither have you."

She whimpered but didn't say anything.

"Then you got scared, didn't you?"

Her head tipped forward, away from his, her shoulders drooped. "Yes," she said.

His fingers continued lavishing their affection on her responsive body. "Why? What were you scared of? Did you really think I only wanted your house?"

Disentangling herself from his hands, she spun and threw her arms around him, buried her face in his neck. "It was kind of about the house," she said through tears. "I mean it was, but it wasn't." Her arms looped tighter, like she never wanted to lose the contact between their bodies. "I was so afraid I wasn't enough to keep you. Like, any minute you'd figure out that there's nothing overtly special about me except for the house so when I thought that was all you wanted, I convinced myself I was right." Her whole body shook with sobs, her skin suddenly covered in goosebumps.

The words reached his ears, but they didn't compute. This amazing, gorgeous, compassionate, interesting, intoxicating woman thought she had nothing to offer him. Leaning away from her, he cradled her face, brushing away the tear-soaked hairs with his thumbs, angled his face to hers and placed a soft kiss on her lips.

"Do you have any idea how much I love you?"

She blinked, focused her eyes on his.

"I don't know if you feel the same about me, but I have to get this off my chest." Unable to resist her slightly puffy lips, he kissed her tenderly, felt her soft breath against his skin. "I have been in love with you since my daughter came home with a handful of flowers that you helped her pick. You had no idea who she was and had no reason to let her do that, aside from the fact that you are who you are."

A few more tears slipped down her cheeks and Rowan kissed them away from one side and then the other. "I didn't want to admit it to myself because I thought I needed to stay mad at you, to punish you for my own disappointment," he said. "But I couldn't do it. And now, to hear you say you thought you brought nothing to the table between us? It was like you were speaking a foreign language. It made no sense in the world."

The look in her eyes reflected back the emotion he felt toward her, and the words stuck in his throat.

"You love me," she said, her voice quiet but confident.

"You have no fucking idea."

Wrapping her arms around his neck, she jumped up and wrapped her legs around his waist, kissing his face with the same abandon he'd been holding back since he saw her at the gallery. She'd opened the door and he was ready to step through it.

"I love you, too," she said between frantic kisses. "I've been in love with you since the night I slept at your house." The heat between her legs pressed into his abdomen as his hands grabbed and held onto her ass. "I am so sorry I was too afraid to say anything." Squeezing her legs tighter around him, she ground her body against his. "I'm sorry I almost wrecked everything."

"You didn't wreck anything," he said, his dick so hard it was painful. "We're here now and we just needed a little time to figure things out." With no reason to slow down, he slid his fingers beneath the bit of fabric that was her underwear, stroking her as he returned her kisses. Tongues clashed and pushed and fought for dominance as his need to be inside her burned higher and hotter with every passing second. "Are we all figured out?"

Her head nodded like a bobble-head doll, and she grabbed two fistfuls of his hair. "Oh my God, Rowan, can you please fuck me now?"

As if he could ever have denied that request. With the woman he loved in his arms, he backtracked through the house until he found her bedroom, tossed her onto the bed and spent the rest of the night making sure she knew exactly how much he loved her.

Sage

DECEMBER OF THAT YEAR

Since moving full-time to Hazelton, Sage's life had become entirely different than the one she'd left behind. Julia and Ty had come out to visit a couple of times over the past five months, scratching the itch of homesickness that threatened every now and then.

Mostly her days had been filled with the last of the work to be done on her little gingerbread house on Orchard Street. Walls had been painted, floors re-carpeted on the first floor, bathrooms updated and stunningly gorgeous. "It doesn't even look like the same house," Julia had gushed to Ty when they first arrived. To Sage, she had said, "I can't believe after all that work, you aren't even going to be living here."

Now, as the last bits of snow flurried around the truck, the bright silver moon reflecting on the snow that had fallen during the day, Rowan turned off the main road into the driveway of the Faraway Inn.

"Whoa," Sage said, eyes wide as the beautiful old building with electric candles burning in every window, and the greenery draped wrap-around porch, came into view.

"It's great, isn't it?" Rowan said, parking the truck and then staring at the scene before them. Pointing off to the right, he said, "That whole part of the building is brand new. That's what Marcus and I, and a whole bunch of other tradesmen, have been working on for the past eight months. They added in a bigger, full-service restaurant and a bar that didn't used to be there, among other things."

As a person who loved what she did for a living, she admired and appreciated the pride he took in his work. "It's amazing," she said. "We should bring Maisie back just to see the lights. She would love it."

Without a word, he leaned over, kissed the soft spot below her ear. "I love you," he said.

"Because I want to bring a six-year-old to see Christmas lights?" she teased.

"Because you are the most amazing woman I've ever known." He squeezed her hand in his. "Oh," he said. "There's one thing I forgot to mention about this inn."

Once she'd gotten over the fact that the inn was owned by Aaron Price, the guitar player for Undercover Angel, one of her absolute favorite bands growing up, she was able to walk somewhat casually into the building.

"Oh," she said, her breath catching in her chest. "That's him." Her heart fluttered and she had to suppress a giggle as Rowan took her hand and they approached Aaron and his wife. Instead of saying words, she stood, mouth agape, and stared.

"It's OK," his wife, Victoria, whispered. "I still get that way about him, and we've been married over a year already."

Jolted back to reality, Sage turned to her and smiled. "Thanks," she said with a slight giggle. "This is actually a little embarrassing."

Utterly charming, Aaron reached out and took her hand, shook it. "It's very nice to finally meet you, Sage." Tilting his head toward Rowan, he said, "This guy talks about you so much, I feel like I already know you."

"Thank you," she said. "And your inn is beautiful." Looking around, the interior was just as elegantly decorated as the outside suggested it would be. People milled around, some sitting at tables in the restaurant, while others hung around the bar, and still others around the tables of hors d'oeuvres.

"While I appreciate the compliment," he said. "This is actually my daughter Alyssa's establishment, and my wife and I merely help out now and again." He pointed to a young woman across the room who turned when she heard her name, flashed a smile and gave a quick wave, then returned to her conversation.

Aaron and his wife continued to mingle with the rest of the guests while Rowan and Sage made their way to the bar. "Hey, strangers," Erin said from her seat beside Marcus. Similar to Sage and Rowan, Erin and Marcus had donned their finest for the inn's first Christmas event. With her hair pinned back on one side, Erin's beauty was on full display and Marcus seemed to be entirely transfixed by her.

Six weeks prior, Sage, Rowan, and Maisie had moved into their own new home together, allowing Sage to rent her house to Erin and Finn, possibly endearing herself to Delores for the rest of her life. The best part of the whole thing was moving Maisie into a north-facing room, and finally being able to give her the yellow walls and bedding she'd always wanted.

"Oh, hey" Marcus finally said, meeting Rowan's eyes. "Hi, guys." Lifting his drink and looking around the room, he said, "Isn't this place awesome?"

The familiar strains of "Jingle Bells" floated through the air from the jazz quartet that had set up somewhere nearby, giving the event an irresistible, cozy Christmas feel.

The four of them spent the evening together, eating, drinking, and laughing. Rowan, Erin, and Marcus shared stories of growing up together that had Sage in stitches. As the night wore on, the music mellowed and Rowan took her by the hand, pulled her to the middle of the living room where couples swayed and danced to the soothing sounds of the quartet.

Erin and Marcus followed.

As they found their space on the floor, Delores and her boyfriend, Adam, walked through the door. Finn was sound asleep in Adam's arms and Maisie's parka covered, pajama-clad form hung behind Delores's legs.

Sage stopped, turning Rowan to see the little troupe. "I think your mom might need you," she said, worry bubbling up as she wondered why they were there and not snug and tucked in at Delores's house for the night.

Rather than be alarmed that they were there, he turned back to her and said, "No, I invited them."

"Rowan, it's way past their bedtime. Maisie's eyes are barely open and look at poor Finn." She attempted to walk toward them, but Rowan refused to let go of her hand, pulling her back to stand beside him.

As her brain scrambled to make sense of what was happening, from across the room, Julia and Ty smiled and waved. Her worlds were colliding and becoming one.

Looking over at the musicians, who stopped playing and gave a little drum trill, Rowan smiled and looked back at Sage. Everyone around them turned to stare as heat burned up Sage's neck into her cheeks.

"May I have your attention just for a minute?" he asked the assembled crowd.

The blood from Sage's brain pooled in her feet, making her dizzy.

Taking a big breath, he said, "First, I want to thank Alyssa, Aaron, and Victoria for such a wonderful night. The inn is amazing, and I wish you all every success."

Everyone clapped and raised their glasses to their hosts. Once it quieted down, Rowan said, "Second, I have a story to share, if you'll indulge me for just a couple minutes."

"Go for it," someone called out from behind Sage. Murmurs of agreement rippled around the room.

"Thank you," Rowan said, then stepped closer to Sage, took her trembling hands and held them in his. Looking her in the eyes, he said, "About four years ago, I found myself, for reasons, needing to move back home with my then two-year-old daughter. It wasn't what I wanted but sometimes life doesn't give us a choice."

Tears welled up along Sage's lower lashes.

"So, we moved back while I saved up money for a new place, one that was the perfect size for the two of us that was close to my mom, to make it easier for her when she would take care of my daughter while I went to work. And then about a year and a half ago, the house I'd been waiting for was about to hit the market. It was the perfect place, small, affordable on one paycheck, and close by."

She blinked and the tears formed little streams over her cheeks.

Erin reached over and handed him a small, square napkin and using the makeshift tissue, he wiped the tears as they fell. "No need for tears. It's not a sad story, baby. It's a great story," he said as he leaned down and placed a kiss against her sweet lips. "It just takes a little while to get to the good parts." He kissed her again, just because he wanted to.

Someone off to her left sniffed which only made Sage's tears fall harder.

"Anyway," he said to the crowd. "Right as I was about to put in my offer, I found out that some woman from the city bought the place right out from underneath us." He paused. "I sort of fell off the emotional cliff. I was hurt and angry and frustrated and every other shitty thing a man could be." Looking her directly in the eye, he said, "And I hadn't even met you yet. I wasn't even willing to give you a chance."

He broke eye contact with her, looking down at their joined hands. "When I started telling you everything that needed to be done in that house, that first night I went over there, I wanted you to see how much work it was going to be and convince you to put it right back on the market and move the hell back to Boston."

It was all in the past, but the memories still stung when they were tinged by his anger. He glided his hand over her exposed arm. "But then I met you, Sage. I spent time with you. I got to know you. Then I got to know you a little better." He traced his finger back up her arm and trailed it under her chin. "Then I got to know you a lot better."

Ripples of laughter rolled through the room. A voice called out, "Yeah, man," causing the crowd, and Sage, to laugh harder.

Reaching into his pocket, Rowan lowered to one knee before her. Whispers of "aww" were everywhere around her. He looked up, held her with the undeniable love in those eyes. "Sage, you have made my life—" He turned to seek out Maisie, who hurried to his side, "our lives," he corrected. "You've made our lives so much better than I could ever have dreamed of. Your energy, your compassion, your love of life is all contagious and I am one hundred percent addicted to you."

Her bottom jaw quivered as he spoke, but she just watched him, tears dripping from her cheeks, landing on her hands which were clasped together in front of her.

"If I ask you with every ounce of love I have in my heart, will you please make an honest man out of me?"

Her face broke into a crying, laughing, smiling mess as she pulled him back to standing then threw her arms around his neck. "Of course I'll marry you," she said. The crowd erupted with shouts and applause, but Sage only had eyes and ears for the man she held. "I love you so much," she said, holding him tighter.

A tug on her dress caught her attention. The crowd hushed again as Sage looked down. Maisie stood staring up at her with huge, round eyes. "Are you going to be my mom for real now?"

"Is that alright with you?" Sage asked, wiping tears from her eyes.

"Yay! Yay! Yay!" Maisie sang, holding onto Sage's dress but jumping up and down. "Yes, I want you to be my mom for real!"

Again, the crowd cheered and several people, including Delores and Erin, sniffed and blew their noses.

As if she wasn't emotional enough, a server appeared with a tray of champagne glasses and one glass of apple juice. They took their glasses and looked on as Aaron called for everyone's attention.

"A toast," he said, raising his glass. "To the happy couple." Smiling at Maisie, he said, "Make that a toast to the happy family."

"Hear, hear," everyone said as glasses clinked all around them.

"Hear, hear," Rowan echoed as he took Sage's champagne and handed both glasses to Julia, who gave Sage's shoulders a squeeze. "Who knew what felt like the worst thing to happen to me would have led to something, *someone*, greater than I ever could have asked for?"

He kissed her gently, then Sage leaned into him. "I love you so much, Rowan Kennedy."

"And I love you, Miss Lowery."

I hope you enjoyed Sage and Rowan's story. If you did, please consider leaving a review at any or all of the usual places. For indie authors, reviews are our bread and butter!

And, if you sign up for my twice-monthly newsletter, Whispers and Works in Progress, you have access to all of my bonus content, including a sweet story about Sage and Rowan and the beginning of their HEA!

Scan the QR code below to sign up for free today!

Afterword

Thank you so much for reading *Picture Me Yours*. Sage and Rowan have been near and dear to my heart for a long time and I'm so happy to let others into their world.

If you enjoyed this story, please consider leaving a rating or review—those mean the world to indie authors like myself. If you really enjoyed this story, please consider recommending it to someone else who might enjoy it!

BOOKS BY E.A. BRADY

Berkshire Romance Series

One Week at the Faraway Inn
Picture Me Yours
Christmas at Whispering Hills

Built to Last Series

Stitches and Sparks
Barstools and Beginnings
Coffee and Kisses

Stand Alone Books

Keep Me Warm: A Christmas Novella
Print Readers – links can be found at home.eabradyauthor.com

About the Author

Despite spending my first few years in New York, I consider myself a New Englander, through and through. My stories are set in fictionalized versions of several of my favorite New England locations and my characters are "real" people who are trying their hardest to make it through to their very own happily ever after.

When I'm not working on new stories, I spend my time working on my Muay Thai round kicks and trying to perfect my left hook. I live in a 130-year-old (haunted?) house with my husband, two amazing kids, and two spoiled tabby cats. I wouldn't have it any other way.